FOREVER
OUR BOYS

FOREVER OUR BOYS
HEIDI MCLAUGHLIN
© 2017

COVER DESIGN: Sarah Hansen - OkayCreations. EDITING: SJS Editorial Services

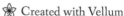 Created with Vellum

For the Beaumont Family

FOREVER
OUR BOYS

1

JENNA

The early morning sunlight peeks through the slats of our bedroom blinds, long before my alarm is set to go off. I snuggle into Jimmy's chest seeking warmth from the cold temperature in our bedroom, because of the central air conditioning. He likes it frigid, while I prefer it a bit warmer. I know it's because he likes it when I use him to keep the chill away, not that I'm complaining. I'm more in love with him today than I was yesterday and the day before.

It's nothing that he does to make me feel this way, other than share my life. From the day he convinced me to marry him, long before he shared the secret he knew he was the father of our daughter, he has showered me with a love I never knew existed, but always wanted. It's the kind of love you read about in romance novels. His love is undying, never wavering, and the most fulfilling emotion I have ever experienced. Don't get me wrong, the bloke can be the biggest arse known to man when he wants to be.

His strong hands and rough stubble against my sensitive neck thwarts my attempt to get out of bed. I curl into him, wishing I didn't have to move, but excited I'm spending the week with my best friends. Josie, Katelyn, and I are headed to the Bahamas for a week of relaxation, spa treatments, and doing nothing but sitting by the pool or beach and sipping on whatever cocktail we want. No phones, no demanding rock-star husbands needing our attention, and no pre-teen drama to fill our days with.

"Don't leave me," he says between the kisses he trails from my ear down the slope of my neck and into the crook of my collarbone. His hand moves over my breast, my hip, and finally settles between my legs, cupping me. "One week without this and I will die," he says in his British accent that can easily bring me to my knees. I would've thought that over the years I would've grown used to it, but I'm not. Every day, I yearn to hear his voice so I can feel my knees weaken and my heart race.

"You'll have your hand," I joke, but he doesn't find the humor it in. One time, we tried to go weeks without sex while he was on tour. The whole band did, but that only lasted until halfway through the second week. None of us were surprised the guys couldn't take it, considering all three of them act as if they're still on honeymoons. Not that any of us are complaining, but it was a nice laugh to see their agony when we walked off the plane. I never did ask Josie and Katelyn how far they made it before their husbands begged for sex. Jimmy and I made it as far as the bathroom before he pulled me into the family stall and bent me over.

But that's him. He's the wild, unconventional one of the group. Liam is laidback while Harrison is reserved. Each guy brings a different dynamic to the table, making 4225 West a success.

"My hand wants your pussy," he says, pushing a finger between my folds. I open for him automatically, letting him have whatever he wants. His ministrations are slow and teasing, knowing full well I'm going to give in and ask him to make love to me again before I leave.

"Jimmy." His name falls breathlessly from my lips. Each time with him is like the first.

"What is it, wifey? Do you have an ache between your legs you need me to take care of?"

He's evil, but I love him and quickly find myself nodding. Only he doesn't roll me to my side or pull me on top of him. He takes his fingers, coated in my juices, and spreads them across my lips before kissing me.

"Fuck, Sweet Lips," he says between his tongue licking away his creation. "I can't get enough of you." Finally, he pulls me on top of him and centers himself between my legs, guiding me down his shaft. My head falls back from the sensation of having him inside of me.

"God, Jimmy, will I ever..." my question ends when he pulls me forward and locks his arms around my back. His legs spread and his hips rise as he pumps into me. I cry out into the pillow beside me, fearful that Eden is awake and can hear us.

She is the only thing we've changed about our love-making. The beauty of Jimmy's job is that when he's home, she's in school and the house is empty. Since moving to California, I haven't worked, except for doing a little bit of marketing for the band and volunteering at Eden's school.

Once she started asking questions, Jimmy and I had to get creative. Bathroom, garage, in the car, any and everywhere we can think where she won't hear us. At night, pillows muffle our sounds while music plays or the television blares. It's only when she's gone to a sleepover do Jimmy and I get crazy.

The pressure he has on my clit and the angle he's hitting my g-spot have me coming undone quickly. He's mastered every position like clockwork, knowing which one he can take his sweet time with and which one he needs to hurry.

"Maybe I don't need to go on vacation," I say as I come down from my high. He chuckles and swats my ass to get me off him. Only I don't move and it was never his intention to let me. Instead, he rolls us onto our sides and my hand instantly covers the scar that is left over from when my ex tried to kill him. His hand cups my cheek and his lips kiss me softly.

"You need this week, Jenna. You all do. You've been catering to us for so long now, doing what we asked, raising our children while we tour, and with everything you've been through, one week will not be the end of us. I can promise you that."

I know he's talking about the miscarriages I have endured. After the third, I stopped counting. I stopped taking tests to see if I was pregnant or counting when I would ovulate. For years, we have wanted another child, but the longer it's taken, the less hope I have.

At first, it didn't make sense. I got pregnant with Eden so easily, even with Jimmy using a condom. So, he tried that again, poking holes in them, thinking that was the trick. It wasn't. We tried IVF. Nothing happened. Every homeopathic remedy we could find, we tried, only to fail.

And each time we did conceive, it was short lived. Each positive test only brought heartache and after a while, I started keeping my miscarriages to myself. I used to confide in Katelyn and Josie. I'd cry for days with Katelyn holding me while Josie would console me over the phone until she could arrive in California. But after the first few losses, I stopped telling them. The look on their faces or the sorrow in their voices was too much to take. For the longest time, they would keep asking if we would have more children and every answer was the same, "We'll see." All while I was dying on the inside.

Jimmy never let me grieve alone though. He was there, holding me and shedding tears with each loss. Promising me he'd do whatever he could to make this happen. He was tested and, of course, his sperm were perfect. I was tested and thought for sure we'd get an answer, but nothing came back as to why I couldn't carry another baby. Another one wasn't in the cards for us.

"I love you." My hands cup his cheek and I move in for a kiss. Our lips linger against each other's until I open my mouth to deepen it. Jimmy pulls my leg up over his hip and enters me again, but this time it's different. There's no urgency in his lovemaking. He's simply reminding me of what I'll be missing for a week and showing me what will be waiting for me when I come home.

"I have to get up," I tell him not long after we've finished round two. He sighs, but rolls out of bed first and pulls on a pair of sweats.

"I'll get Eden, you shower." And just like that, he's out of our room and down the hall, knocking on our daughter's door. Jimmy learned a long time ago to knock before entering. He once saw her posing in front of the mirror with only her bikini on and threatened to ground her for a month even though she wasn't doing anything wrong.

After I shower and finish packing, I head downstairs to find Jimmy and Eden sitting at the kitchen island eating breakfast in silence. Right away, I know something is wrong, but I'm afraid to ask.

"Mum, you can't leave me with Dad," Eden says in her adopted accent. I thought for sure she would speak American, but considering she spends the summers in England, I'm not surprised she has a bit of a British tongue to her dialect. "Mum, please?" The look on her face is one of desperation.

"Why not?"

"Because she wants to invite a bloody bloke over and I ain't having it."

"Not just a boy, Daddy, all my friends. I can't help that my friends are boys too."

I look from Jimmy to Eden and crack a smile. Any reservations I had about leaving are gone. These two need a week alone together. But still, I offer a suggestion. "How about I call my mom and invite her, yeah?"

Jimmy spits his coffee back into his mug and glares at me, then Eden. "You'd really do that to your old man, Little One? Make him spend a week with your granny?"

Still to this day my parents and Jimmy don't always see eye to eye, but they get along. I don't know if it stems from him getting me pregnant during a one-night stand, the fact that he took me away to get married, or that he's a musician. He's cordial though and welcomes them warmly when they come to visit.

Eden laughs, knowing full well that her father would rather die than spend the week with my mother.

"Tell you what, Jimmy. Let Eden have her friends over as planned and ask Elle and Quinn to come over to help you babysit."

At the sound of Quinn's name, Eden's eyes light up. This isn't lost on Jimmy in the least.

"Er, fuck no," he says, pushing away from the island. "I'll bloody well look after everyone myself." He storms out of the kitchen, muttering who knows what. Eden and I both laugh uncontrollably when we hear the bedroom door shut.

"That was brilliant, Mum."

I shake my head. "You listen good, Eden. Do not do anything to piss off your father. He's having a hard enough time with you growing up. The last thing you want is to find yourself locked in your room for a week."

"He wouldn't."

"I would, so don't even try it," Jimmy says as he comes back into the room. "Come on, let's go. We need to take your mum to the airport to meet your Aunt Katelyn, then you and I are going to have a long father-daughter chat on the way to school."

"I'm going to die," she mutters, sliding off the stool.

"No, you're not, Eden. I'll only be gone for a week."

"A week in the life of a teenager is like a year. You're killing me," she huffs on her way out to the car. Jimmy grabs my hand and pulls me back.

"I'm going to die a very painful death, but I'm happy you're having a vacation and I love you."

"Now I know where Eden gets all her drama from."

"From me, of course," he says, winking. "Now get your arse in the car, Sweet Lips."

2

JOSIE

My hand reaches for the worn-out button on my alarm clock, patting it a few times until the annoying beep ceases. Whoever created this jarring sound is made of evil. The noise is meant to rouse me from my sleep; instead, it shocks my heart into a faster rhythm and scares the ever-loving crap out of me each time. Even when I'm already awake.

Liam adjusts behind me, showing me that even after all these years, he's still eager for me. His lips are on my bare shoulder while his fingers dig into the curvature of my hip, pulling me to an angle that is easily accessible for him. There has never been any doubt in my mind, Liam and I were made for each other. One simple touch, a lingering kiss, or a lustful look from him and I'm ready.

I roll over and face him, letting my fingers trace the tattoo of my nickname, and then onto Noah and Betty

Paige's names. The three loves of his life permanently etched over his heart.

"Are you sure you want to leave me?" he asks as he moves over to my pillow.

"It's only for a week," I remind him. I play with his five o'clock shadow. He never balked when I told him that Katelyn, Jenna, and I would take a wives' week in the Bahamas, at least not until last night. He seems to forget that he leaves me often, and each time is worse than the earlier tour. I love having him home, waking up next to him every morning, and falling asleep nestled in his arms. When he's on tour, I feel lost and alone. I must find things to occupy my time so I'm not constantly texting or calling him, or counting down the days until Paige and I are with him. The cycle of longing starts over again once I leave him.

I thought that my feelings would level off over the years, but that has never been the case. Each day, I find I love him more.

"I know I'm gone a lot, but the thought of you leaving me... it's killing me, Josie."

My hand moves from his cheek and into his hair, using the motion to pull him closer until his lips touch mine. My skin pebbles instantly as his hand moves under the comforter and pulls my leg over this hip.

"Can I make love to you?" he breaks away from our kiss long enough to ask me the silliest question ever.

"You never have to ask me. I'm yours, always."

He pushes my hair behind my ear and leans

forward, brushing his lips against mine. "You're forever my girl, Jojo."

He bites down on my shoulder as he enters me with slow and steady thrusts, never taking his eyes off mine, even as mine threaten to close, I find myself needing to see him and fight to keep them open.

His lips hover over mine, breathing the same air as me. I moan and he captures my lips, swallowing each sound until he pulls away. "Shh," he says, reminding me our daughter is down the hall.

I do my best to keep quiet, but it's near impossible with him. He knows this and by the smirk spreading across his lips, he's enjoying the torment. I could take revenge and climb on top of him, but I'm enjoying this position. It's bringing us closer and seems more intimate even though I can't touch him like I want.

Liam moves his hips faster, hitting my spot perfectly. I'm forced to bite the inside of my cheek to keep my sounds at a minimum, but the torture is too much to bear.

"Scream into the pillow," he says, before he flips me onto my stomach and pins my legs together by his. "So fucking tight," I hear him say as he enters me from behind. From this angle, it only takes a few thrusts until I'm falling over the edge and calling out his name. Everything from me is muffled into the pillow, but he's sure to moan into my ear. It turns me on even more, knowing that I make him feel this way, that I'm the one who makes him lose control. I spent far too long in the beginning of our marriage wondering if I was enough for him. Each time he tried to show me or I would finally accept I am everything he wants, something would happen and I'd be back at zero, trying to piece everything together.

Liam grunts out his orgasm and falls on top of me, breathing heavily. He stays there for a few seconds before rolling over.

"Stay home," he says, rising onto his elbow. He peppers my back with kisses and small nips that he replaces by his tongue to take the sting away. "We can send Paige to your parents and fuck all week long."

"Don't you have songs to write? Music to produce?"

"Nah," he says, shaking his head.

I laugh, knowing full well that they're behind schedule and were meant to deliver new music to the label last month. Liam, being the primary songwriter, has writer's block and everything he's tried to clear his mind, hasn't worked.

"Besides, we're flying to see Noah on Sunday," I point out.

He shrugs, but I know damn well he would not miss Noah's game. When Liam is home, his children, regardless of their age, are his priority. He doesn't miss anything that Betty Paige has going on or any of Noah's games, flying to wherever he's playing.

"You talk a big game, Mr. Page, but I see right through you."

His hand smacks my ass, causing me to yelp. "You know how I get when you call me Page."

"I know and I love it, but I really do need to get dressed."

"I don't like you flying by yourself."

I don't like it either, but it made more sense for Katelyn and Jenna to fly on the band's private jet than it did for me to use it alone, and the thought of either of us flying to each other didn't seem like a good use of our time.

"I'll be fine. I'm in first class, drinking my way to the Bahamas, chatting with whoever is sitting next to me."

Liam groans. He's already told me not to talk to any men—he doesn't trust them.

"You're killing me, woman."

"You love me," I remind him.

He rests his head on my pillow and pushes my hair away from my face. "I love you more than words can express, Josie. You're my life. You, Noah, and Betty Paige... I am nothing without you."

"Liam..." When he says things like this, my heart soars with so much love. For every day that we've been together, the days we weren't still weigh heavily on my mind. They were more present when Paige was an infant. I could see it in his eyes when he'd talk to Noah. Liam missed everything. Thinking back, I wish I had just told him in the message that I was pregnant, but I wanted him to call me back. I wanted him to tell me why he left me. "I love you," I say, kissing him. "You're my life and the best damn father to our children."

"Mom? Dad?" Betty Paige's voice at the door has us

scrambling to cover up. We are long past the time when she used to crawl into bed with us and we were forced to sleep in clothes. There was a time when I would wear a nightgown to bed, only to have it on the floor within seconds. After a while, I gave up until Paige started coming into our bedroom in the middle of the night. Liam grumbled a lot back in those days.

Liam sits up and puts a pillow over his crotch. I laugh and quickly slip my bathrobe on before crawling back into bed.

"Come in, Paige," Liam says, his voice is a bit gruff as if he wants her to believe we were sleeping. I stifle a laugh, which earns me the classic side eye.

Betty Paige enters, dressed and ready for school. I glance at the clock and realize that it's later than I had thought. "I was just wondering if you were coming downstairs this year or do I have to make my own breakfast?"

"You're old enough to make your own breakfast, Paige," I say, slightly irritated.

She shrugs. "But Daddy is home."

Yes, he is, and that means when he's home, he treats her like a baby, waiting on her hand and foot. It bothers me, but there isn't anything I can do about it. He thinks he must be like this because he missed chunks of time with her while he was on tour.

I shake my head and get out of bed, heading straight for the shower. He can deal with her and the attitude that comes with her.

Standing under the hot spray, I try to recall what

Noah was like at this age. The gap between a pre-teen to teen was filled with sports and two fathers that never let him act like a brat. Even with Liam back, Nick was never far away, and was always present in Noah's life. If he couldn't talk to Liam about something, he went to Nick. I know that hurt Liam, but he never let Noah onto the fact.

Still, Betty Paige pushes the envelope because Liam lets her. She's not like this when he's not home. She's independent and eager to help around the house. But when her father is home... Lord help any man she decides to date, especially if it's Mack Ashford, Nick and Aubrey's son. I have a feeling if their shy flirting turns into something serious, Liam will have a heart attack.

When I get out of the shower, music wafts through the speakers in our house and the smell of French toast fills the air. I use these last few minutes to finish packing. I won't need much—bathing suits, cover-ups, and a few dresses. The girls and I don't plan to do much except lie by the pool and relax.

"Smells good," I say as I enter the kitchen. Liam gives me a quick kiss and goes back to tending to the skillet.

"Paige wanted French toast."

I nod, and keep my comments to myself. There is no use fighting with him about her, especially when I'm about to leave. The phone breaks me from my thoughts and I rush to answer it without looking at the caller ID.

"Hello?"

"Hey, Mom."

"Noah, hi." I glance quickly at the time on the microwave and realize it's very early in Portland, where he lives. "Are you okay?"

"Yeah, I have practice in a bit, but I wanted to call and tell you to have a good time. You deserve this vacation. You all do, actually."

"Thank you. I'm sorry I'm going to miss your game, but Dad and Paige will be there."

"I don't want to go," Paige yells out. She hates football, or more so she hates that her brother's games take up her weekends right now. Not that she has a social life or anything.

"Don't listen to her. She's moody this morning."

"It's fine. Are you all packed?"

I laugh at his question. "Listen to you, acting like a parent. Is there something you want to tell me?"

"Hell, no. No kids for me, Mom."

My heart breaks a little. Not that I want to rush him into anything, even though I'd love having a baby around the house again, but he needs to be with someone that deserves his love. His current girlfriend, while she's beautiful, I'm not a big fan. I do my best to hide my feelings when she's around.

We talk for a few more minutes until it's time for Paige to go to school. Liam hands me a paper bag with my name written on the front.

"What's this?"

"Breakfast for your flight. If you're ready to leave me for a week, we ought to get you to the airport.

Unless you plan to stay?" he asks, waggling his eyebrows.

"You wish!"

He does wish and by the look on his face, he's crushed that he's not enough to keep me home. He is, but I don't want to let the girls down.

3

KATELYN

The sand is cold against my bare feet, and the cool breeze makes me shiver. I should've changed into something warmer before I decided to trek out in the wee hours of the morning to watch Harrison surf. It's not often that I do this, but something woke me and told me that I needed to be out here. I'm thankful that I am.

Harrison glides over the waves, holding his balance until he's safely back on shore, only to paddle back out and wait for the next crest to form. Moving to California has been a good thing for us. At first, I balked. I didn't want to leave Beaumont, leave Mason. The thought of not visiting Mason's grave whenever I wanted, gutted me, but I had to do what was right for Harrison because he had done so much for me. When Quinn chose to move here for school, I knew Harrison wanted to be near his son. Not to mention his mom and sister live here. But it wasn't until Elle said she was going to enroll at UCLA did I finally agree. The only problem with that is it left Peyton all alone. Even with her choice to attend school in Chicago, I haven't fully accepted that my girls aren't together. The twins are twenty now and vastly different than what I expected them to be.

It's funny. When they were born, Mason and I used to lie on our bed with them between us and discuss what we thought they'd be when they grew up. I had these grand ideas of the girls being doctors or lawyers while Mason said that Peyton would be the first female coach in the NFL because he was going to teach her everything he knew. He would've, if given the chance, and she would be on her way, but that's not her path. His little football player strives to be on the sidelines with live reporting or broadcasting for big sports channels.

Peyton and Mason had a bond that I could never compete with. From the time she was a newborn, until he died, she was his shadow. When I couldn't calm her down, he could. When she was hurt, she only wanted her dad. After Mason died, I thought she would crumble, but Liam was there to hold her up, and with Liam came Harrison. He has a bond not only with Peyton, but Elle as well, that will never be broken. People who don't know us, would never suspect he isn't their father.

With Elle, I thought she'd be the one to go to school and become a cheerleader or study fashion merchandising. She was always my little fashionista. Elle was the one who always butted heads with her sister about her sports attire and how it didn't match her stylish clothes. So, it shocked us when she announced that she was going to school to learn business management with a minor in music so she can become an agent or manager.

Harrison and I were surprised, but it made sense. Quinn, of course, followed in his father's footsteps and after everything the band has gone through, we figured that Elle doesn't want the same thing to happen to her brother.

Very slowly, the sun begins to rise, casting a beautiful glow over the Pacific Ocean and Harrison. He's my sunshine, the bright light that kept me from the dark tunnel I was heading for after Mason died. Harrison was the last person I wanted to let into my life, and I did everything to prove that he wasn't the man he claimed to be. I was wrong each time. Each day I have been incredibly thankful that I was. I don't know where I'd be, mentally, if it weren't for him. He saved me and I know I did the same for him.

Quinn is my son, in every sense of the word. I am the mom that he never had and he's the son I always dreamed of having. To say he's a mama's boy, even though we came into each other's life when he was eight, is an understatement. He comes to me with his questions, concerns, and problems. I know all about his girlfriends and the older women that continue to throw themselves at him when he has a gig. Quinn shares everything with me, even a few things I don't want to know about and need a few minutes to process, but I'll always be there for him.

The relationship between Quinn and the twins is as one would suspect. They argue like siblings. He protects them as big brothers do, and all three support each other one hundred percent.

Later this morning, Harrison will take me to the airport where I'll meet Jenna and board a private flight to the Bahamas to meet Josie for a week of rest and relaxation. I miss Josie and haven't seen her in a few months. That was another downfall of moving to California, leaving my best friend. Josie and I have been friends for as long as I can remember. I was there when Liam left her and she was there when Mason died. We've been through everything together, from broken hearts, the birth of our children, and the return of Liam into our lives. There wasn't a day I didn't see her until we moved.

When we first arrived here, I was okay. It felt like a vacation, but as the weeks passed, my heart started breaking. I missed Josie dearly. Phone calls weren't cutting it and I quickly found myself traveling back to Beaumont or begging her to come out here. Josie traveling out here was much easier. Despite their rocky start, she has a good relationship with her mother-in-law, Bianca, who is living in her old childhood home.

Harrison catches another wave and weaves in and out of it until it drops him back at the shore. Then, he looks up and sees me sitting in the sand. I'm too far away to see his expression, but I imagine his bright smile matches mine. I never thought I'd fall in love again, but then he walked into my life with a bouquet of flowers, only knowing it was my first Christmas without my husband, and cemented himself in my life. I only looked back once and that was a mistake. From that point forward, I have vowed to love him with everything I am.

He stands in the surf and removes the top of his wet suit before he picks up his board and comes toward me. The water dripping down from his hair glistens on his tanned and toned chest. Harrison slams his board into the sand next to me, then shakes his hair over me, causing me to scream. He uses this to his advantage and falls to his knees, pushing me back in the sand, and hovers over me.

Our eyes are pinned on each other, both of us smiling.

"I love you," he tells me. This isn't out of the blue or some random act of love. He tells me every day as soon as he sees me. It's not "good morning" or "here's your coffee." The first words he speaks are about love, and each morning, I fall more in love with him.

"I love you too," I say as I pull him down on top of me and kiss him. I don't care that his suit is wet and that it's cold out; being this close to him is something I can never get enough of.

Harrison tries to move to the side, to not put all his weight on me, but I refuse to let him move. I'm not going to see him for a week, and one might think it's not a big deal, especially because he tours with the band. For me, it's an eternity. When he would tour, I had the kids to occupy my time even though I was a wreck, waiting to hear from him every second of the day. I tried not to be a needy partner, but that notion went out the door very quickly.

Now that the kids are grown, I can tour with him even though it's slightly awkward being the only wife on the road with the guys. Still, I don't pass up the opportunity. Being away from him is my least favorite thing in life.

My hand slips between his torso and into his tight shorts. The wet suit makes it almost impossible for me to grip his shaft. His eyes roll back briefly until his senses catch up with him. He pulls my shorts aside and presses his thumb over my bud as his mouth crashes down onto mine. Our tongues tangle as our hands bring us pleasure. With my free hand, I work the zipper on his suit, pulling it down far enough so I can get my hand in there to pull down his shorts. Last night, he made love to me until neither of us could move, but knowing that I'm leaving him for a week, I need him again.

Harrison sits back on his knees and pushes his shorts down enough to escape the tight confines. He leans forward, hovering over me and kissing me deeply while his fingers pull my shorts aside so he can enter me. I open my mouth to cry out, but his mouth swallows my cries, preventing the houses around us from hearing me.

My nails dig into his back, clutching him to my chest as he tries to be discreet about what we're doing. He looks at me and pulls his lower lip between his teeth. It's his tell that he's close. My back arches when his thumb presses on my swelling bud.

"Give it to me one more time," he whispers into my ear, paying homage to the hours and hours we spent last night and into the morning making love. He wanted to make sure I didn't forget him in the week I'd be gone. "God, baby, I can feel you."

Harrison changes angles and thrusts faster until my orgasm peaks. He follows quickly, grunting through his release and collapsing on top of me, panting.

"Are you getting old on me?" I ask, poking fun at our slight age difference.

Harrison chuckles and bites my neck. "Never." He rolls us onto our sides and discreetly pulls his shorts up. I glance around and see if anyone else is on the beach. There's another surfer down the way, but too far away to see what we've been doing. This isn't the first time we've had sex outside. In fact, after the first time on his motorcycle so many years ago, it's been sort of our thing.

We both rest on our elbows and stare into each other's eyes. Every day is like we're falling in love all over again. He pushes my hair behind my ear and gives me a quick kiss. "I'm going to miss you."

"One week."

He rolls his eyes. "One week of men looking at you, thinking they stand a chance."

I shake my head and place my lips on his chest where he has our names tattooed over his heart. "Never. You own me," I tell him. "Heart and soul."

"We should probably get inside and shower. We are going to hit traffic on the way to the airfield. Unless you want to stay home with me?"

"And miss all those half-naked men on the prowl for a week-long hook-up? No way," I say as I stand up in a rush and run toward our house. Harrison is hot on my tail and catches me as I reach our patio. He grabs me and I squeal.

"I think I need to fuck those thoughts out of you," he says, carrying me into the house.

"Yes, please!"

4

JENNA

"Should we check in or wait... for Josie?" My words trail off as I step into The Cove and onto the marble floor. I can feel my mouth drop open as I take in the magnitude of this hotel.

"The guys weren't kidding," Katelyn says.

"No, they weren't."

The guys, being our husbands, insisted that we turn our girls' week away into seven days of pampering. Despite our best attempts at finding a nice hotel with a nice beach, the guys became adamant that we treat ourselves, as a gift from them. As a thank you for taking care of them, their families, and lives while they're on tour.

For a month or longer, the guys bickered about where we should stay, what we should do, and even as to where we would go. It came down to Betty Paige and Eden suggesting that everyone's recommendations for a hotel be put into a hat. Whatever name was drawn would be the place that we would stay.

Of course, arguing ensued about who would draw a name because in all honesty, Jimmy, Liam, and Harrison are children in adult-sized bodies and they can't agree on a single thing most of the time.

In the end, Paige drew the name because she was the youngest in the room, and all Eden wanted to do was go surfing; our indecisiveness was taking up valuable wave time.

And that is how we ended up standing in this grandiose lobby, with our mouths hanging open, acting like we've never seen anything like this before.

"I should've come here on my honeymoon," Katelyn says, causing me to laugh.

"Did you and Harrison recently tie the knot and not tell us?" I ask.

Katelyn looks over and smiles at me. My heart beats fast, thinking that one of my best friends would take the plunge without having our family there to witness the act.

"No," she says with a devilish grin. "Harrison and I are extremely happy with the way things are now." Katelyn steps forward, dragging her suitcase behind her as the sound of her flip-flops echoes throughout the lobby. It's a sound I hate, but have grown to tolerate it with Eden wearing them every day.

I follow her quickly toward the registration desk, curious of what has been booked for us.

27

"Good afternoon, Mrs. James, Mrs. Davis," the clerk says before either of us can give our names.

I glance quickly at Katelyn who rolls her eyes. "I'm sorry, but how do you know who we are?" she asks. "Surely, our reservations are under a different name?"

"Most of us in Atlantis are big fans," the clerk tells us as her fingers move wildly over the keyboard. "When we found out you were coming, we all became very excited."

"How does one find out?" I ask.

The clerk stops, but doesn't make eye contact with us, meaning our question goes unanswered. Great. Perfect. No privacy.

All thoughts of being hounded run through my mind. We were probably better off bringing the guys; this way we'd have security with us and people wouldn't dare try to ask us questions.

The young woman slides our keycards to us and rambles instructions on how to find our room and our private cabana. She goes into detail about our itinerary, telling us when our trip to the spa is, the day we'll visit the dolphins, and our Island tours. "Here is a list of restaurants, and when you're ready to go to Aquaventure, let us know. The bellhop will be here shortly to help you."

"Thank you," we both say. We step away from the desk and wait for the bellhop to take us to our room. I have every doubt in my mind that I will get lost if I try to find my room by myself. I only need to be shown once, maybe twice, before I can find my way there.

"That had to be Eden's idea," I say, looking over the flyer for Aquaventure.

"Do you think we should've brought the kids?" Katelyn asks.

I adamantly shake my head. "First off, you don't have small children. Yours are grown and out of the house; why on Earth would you want to vacation with them?"

Katelyn opens her mouth to stay something, but closes it quickly.

"Second, we need this! Look at this place, Katelyn. They picked it for us because they love us and know we need a break. I do wish they were here though."

"We could call them?" she says, but I shake my head. "I know you're right. I'm feeling—"

"Like you have an empty nest?"

She looks at me wide eyed. "Yes. I hate that the kids aren't together. Mostly, Peyton though; she's alone in Chicago and I worry about her. I'm constantly watching the news... and I hate the news, Jenna. There is so much crime. Harrison tells me that Peyton is fine, and that she'll call if she needs anything, but I still worry."

The bellhop whistles his way toward us. "Hello, would you like me to show you to your room?"

"Yes, that would be much appreciated," I say as I reach for my bag. He takes it from my hand, and reaches for Katelyn's too. We fall in step behind him, and I quickly find myself chuckling because our bellhop looks a bit disjointed with his arms extended back, pulling two suitcases.

Katelyn steps forward and slides our key in and opens the door. In my head, angels are singing as we step into our penthouse suite. The windows are open, letting the sound of the ocean wash over the room.

"Sorry," the bellhop says, as he rushes past us to close the window. "Usually these are closed to keep the cool air inside."

"It's okay," I tell him. I hand him his tip and thank him. Once he's gone, I look at Katelyn and laugh. Our suite is beautiful, but in 4225 West colors.

"We can't get away," she says, trailing her fingers along the black leather sofa with red and white accent pillows.

"They planned this," I say.

"You know they did. They somehow rigged this hotel being drawn."

Nothing surprises me when it comes to the guys. Katelyn and I tour the rest of the suite. It's huge, with a full dining room table that seats eight. Each room has a king-sized bed, and overlooks the ocean. In fact, every space in the room has a view of the ocean.

"I'm never going to want to leave," I mumble.

"And yet, we live on the beach."

Katelyn's right. We have this luxury at our finger-tips, yet here we are, vowing to never leave paradise.

"What time is Josie supposed to arrive?" I ask as I continue to stare out at the perfect sandy beach and blue waters.

"Not for another couple of hours. Should we visit our cabana?"

"Yeah, we should."

We change quickly and follow the signs that lead to the private beach. We have a cabana reserved for the duration of our stay. As soon as we sit down, a waitress appears, out of thin air.

"What can I get for you ladies?"

"Can you surprise us?" Katelyn asks. "We'll take whatever is your special drink for the day."

"And some fruits? Maybe an appetizer tray?" I add.

"I'll be right back," she tells us, leaving us to get situated. Every cabana here is different. Some have a double lounge bed, while others have a sofa and chairs. I don't know who requested what in ours, whether it was one of the husbands or the staff here, but it's very accommodating with three single lounge beds, and tables between for us to set our stuff down.

Katelyn dumps her bag onto one of the beds. Sunglasses, cell phone, and three books spill out.

"Prepared, I see," I laugh at her pile.

"What? I didn't want to get bored."

I spread my arms out wide. "How can you get bored here? I mean, look at this place."

"And the eye candy," she says, nodding toward the side of the pool where two guys are looking at us. I quickly duck behind the curtain and stifle my laugh.

"No way," I tell her quietly. "I know you won't even entertain them."

She shrugs. "I mean, we're here and—"

"Katelyn Powell-James, I do not believe a single word coming out of your mouth right now." I pick up one of her books and pretend to throw it at her. A name on the inside catches my attention. Mason's name is etched onto the paper. It's faded, but still there.

I'm afraid to look at her face out of fear we've chosen the wrong week to get away. It's been so long since he passed that dates slip by, and I find myself forgetting to remember him.

The white gauzy material that makes up the curtains sways with the slight breeze we have, brushing against my skin. I smile at the thought that Mason is here, especially when it seems Katelyn needs him right now.

That's why she keeps asking if the husbands should've come. It's something I'm going to have to ask Josie when she gets here. The last thing I want to do is feel like I must walk around on eggshells because I might say something stupid.

"I'm going to test out the water," I tell her, motioning over my shoulder. I quickly ditch my cover-up and straighten out my bikini. "Wanna come?"

Katelyn hesitates for a minute before nodding. She ditches her cover-up and reaches for my hand. Together, we walk to the edge, away from the two men that she saw earlier.

"Sharks," she says, nodding to the guys.

I glance around the resort and see that we're surrounded. "They're everywhere."

"And will turn into vultures once word spreads that we're here."

She's right. As much as I want to say no one cares that we are here, the truth is, they do, or will once they find out. To us, we're the wives of men that entertain millions with their music. We're the ones doing their wash, making their dinner, and playing dad to their children when they're out on tour. But to others, we're the ticket. Many think they can get in good with us, and that we'll invite them over and let them party with the guys.

But it doesn't work that way, at least not with Josie, Katelyn, or me. We're a closed-off, tight-knit family with steel doors and shutters. Even the kids experience their own turmoil because of who their fathers are.

Eden is very cautious about who she brings home, and often chooses to spend time at her friend's house over ours. I hate that for her, but I understand. Jimmy doesn't. He wants her home, away from the temptations of the world. Even when she has a surfing competition, he's there, and if he can't be, a bodyguard is. Eden is protected at all times. The last thing he wants is for his career to interfere with hers.

Still, it's happened. Her competitors accuse judges of giving her better scores because of who her father is, which would make sense if her father could surf as well as she can. Now, if Harrison was her father, I could understand, but not Jimmy. He has no influence over the judging of a surfing competition. What's he going to do, offer them a signed CD?

33

Knowing my husband, he would try, if Eden wasn't any good, but that's not the case. She's one of the best on the junior circuit and keeps telling us that she plans to be a professional surfer by the time she's seventeen. Most of the time I want to tell her no, that she needs an education, but can't. I don't want to be the parent that limits their child, but also don't want to turn my back on an opportunity.

Jimmy blames me. Saying that if I hadn't been adamant that we move to California, none of this would've happened. I, of course, remind him this is payback for knocking me up in the first place.

5

JOSIE

The last time I flew commercial, I had flown out to Los Angeles under the guise that I was attending a convention on floristry when in fact I was going to see Liam. I sat in coach, crammed between two men who were conducting business together, and using me as an extra tray to hold their papers. I was too nervous to say anything, even though I wanted to switch seats. There was something about being on the edge that afforded me the ability to escape, even though I knew there wasn't anywhere for me to go.

The entire flight to Los Angeles, I had to talk myself into following through with my plan to go see Liam and demand an explanation. I wanted to know everything, and yet I didn't. There hadn't been a day in the ten years that he was gone that I hadn't thought about him, even when I didn't want to, but never in a million years did I expect him to show up in Beaumont after Mason died.

That day in his penthouse was a defining moment for me. When I let Liam kiss me, I knew I couldn't marry Nick, no matter how much I loved him. I would've been lying to Nick when I took my vows. That wouldn't have been fair to anyone involved.

Now here I am again, flying commercial but as Liam's wife, and this time in first class. The man next to me is reading a rag mag and laughing. There used to be a time when I would see one of those and break down in tears. Liam would be plastered on the front with a random woman and an unfavorable headline. It took years before I could ignore the magazines. The local store saw how I reacted when I got to the checkout, or noticed that Mason would turn the publications around so we wouldn't have to look. It didn't take long before the store refused to stock any magazine with his picture on it. Liam didn't just leave Mason, Katelyn, and me behind. He left us all. The whole town felt his departure, and when he became famous, most expected him to waltz back into town and sweep me off my feet.

Everyone that is, except for me. I knew Liam wasn't ever coming back. If he didn't have the heart to return my calls after he left, there was no way he'd show his face in Beaumont again. That all changed when Mason died. I had so many thoughts and emotions going through me, but not even one of them was about Liam. Not once did I think that Liam would show up or that he'd even know about Mason. But he did, and his arrival changed everything.

The man next to me shakes the paper closed, and that's when I spot my son and his girlfriend on the front page. My stomach twists into knots as my heart beats a bit faster. As Noah's mother, I've worked to protect him from the limelight, only for him to thrust himself right into it. Deep down, I had hoped he would've chosen a different career path, but he didn't. He opted to follow in his father's footsteps in a roundabout sort of way.

Everyone, Nick included, thought that Noah would accept one of the many scholarship offers he received. One of the best pitchers in the region, Noah was well sought after. The agent that wanted to sign him hours after he turned eighteen told Liam that Noah was a top draft pick, likely number one, but that wasn't what Noah wanted. He wanted football, but the sport he loved didn't necessarily love him back.

Many college football coaches wouldn't talk to Noah. At first, I thought it was because of Liam and forced him to make some calls to find out. The truth was, Noah didn't fit into their system or hadn't done anything as a standout player to get their attention. Noah took the news with an upbeat attitude and made his own call.

Years ago, while the band was on tour and we were with them, we'd do the tourist thing. We'd check out different sites and turn each stop into an adventure. One such stop brought us to the University of Notre Dame where Noah fell in love with the Irish pride.

That was the one call he made, asking the coach if he could try out for the team.

Liam and Nick didn't have the heart to tell him that even if he did make the team, he'd be sitting on the bench. At best, he'd be the third or fourth-string quarterback and would only see field time during practices, if that.

Instead, Liam helped Noah pack and we drove him to Indiana. While I unpacked his room, Noah and Liam went and met with the coach. I cried the whole way home, worrying about my son. It didn't take long for the call to come from Noah, letting us know that he was the starting quarterback. I made Liam fly me to his game, where I sat proudly at the fifty-yard line, cheering Noah on.

Noah played all four years for the Irish. Even though pro scouts highly recruited him, he was loyal to his coach and the program. Of course, it helped that the coach gave Noah a full ride by his sophomore year. Something Noah never stopped earning.

The Portland Pioneers, an expansion team, drafted him. Once again, I found myself wondering if Noah was making the right choice by signing the contract. My feelings never mattered, but I wanted him to be happy.

Until this week, I have never missed a game, and believe me, knowing my son is playing is enough for me to want to stay home. Except, Liam and Noah won't allow it. They say I need this break, although I'm not sure that I do. It's not like I live a high-stressed life or never get to see my friends. It's true, that living away from Katelyn and Jenna is hard, but I have Whimsicality to keep me busy, and Betty Paige.

Still, seeing Noah on the cover of this magazine with his girlfriend makes me wish for a time when women were the farthest thing from his mind and his idea of dating was taking Quinn, Peyton, and Elle to the drive in where all their friends piled into the back of his truck.

But times changed, and now he's with Dessie, and as much as I try to like her, I can't. I've tried desperately to welcome her into our home, but something about her I can't quite put my finger on. I don't know if it's because of her job and my experiences with Liam or because of the way she latches onto Noah when I'm around. It could also be that she's always sullen when we go out to dinner after Noah's games. It's as if my presence bothers her.

I try to look at the headline, but the gentleman next to me stuffs the paper into the front pocket. Only the top of Noah's head is showing, which makes my fingers itch. I could tap him on the shoulder and ask him to borrow it, but I'm afraid what the story might say.

Fortunately, the captain comes on, alerting us that we're starting our descent. I peek out the window, only to see nothing but water. I've mentioned to Liam a few times that the band should do a fan cruise. Of course, I said this in front of Jimmy who I knew would be up for it. Liam, not so much, and Harrison was on the fence. Liam doesn't like the idea that fans would have access to him twenty-four seven. I told him it wouldn't be like that, but he doesn't believe me. I figure once I can lay out the details and show him we'd have our own private space that fans couldn't access, he might go for it.

As soon as the plane lands, the man next to me is up and out of his seat. His newspaper is still in the seat pocket, beckoning me to take it. I reach for it, only to hesitate long enough that the passenger behind me motions for me to go forward. It's best I leave it there. The less I know from the tabloids the better off I am. I have learned that lesson the hard way.

There's a car waiting for me as soon as I step off the plane. The sign the driver holds up says, "Mrs. Liam Page." I can't help but laugh at how over the top Liam is sometimes. There are times when he wants us to be completely anonymous, and other times when he wants to flaunt it. This is one of those moments.

The driver takes my bag and helps me into the back of the car, where a present waits for me. I open it, tossing aside the wrapping and the lid, only to find a two-piece bathing suit with Liam's autograph imprinted on the fabric. The card attached reads, "To the love of my life. Enjoy your week with the girls. You deserve it. Paige and I will hold down the fort. Oh, and be sure to wear the bikini. Every man needs to know who you belong to. Love, Liam."

The bikini is white with red piping and black letters. I shake my head at the thought of wearing this, but know that Liam will expect pictures. I send him a quick text letting him know I've landed, I have my present, and I love him.

The drive to the hotel is quick and a bit terrifying considering the driver is weaving in and out of traffic. I close my eyes too many times to count, praying that I'll make it to the hotel in one piece. I breathe a sigh of relief when the car stops and my door opens.

"Mrs. Page," the bellhop says as he reaches for my hand. I want to correct him, telling him that my name is Westbury, but I let it go. This is Liam's doing because he knows that Page pulls more weight. "Your friends are in the cabana waiting for you. I've been directed to escort you there immediately."

"What about my bags?"

"I'll take care of them," he tells me as he guides me into the lobby and down the hall. My heels clank against the marble, tempting me to take them off, but he seems to be in a hurry so I follow along until we're back outside and he's pointing to a cabana. "You'll find the rest of your party there."

The pool is crowded. The laughter and splashing brings me back to a time when Liam and I used to do that. It seems that relaxation weekends have gotten away from us the older Betty Paige gets. Liam never wants to leave her because he's gone so much. I get it, but a weekend away with my hubby would be nice every now and again.

I find Jenna and Katelyn, with drinks in their hands, staring straight out into the pool. "Who are you guys staring at?" I ask.

Both squeal and jump up, wrapping me in their arms. I've tried not to let the fact that they don't live in Beaumont get me down, but feeling their arms around me now, makes me long to live near them again. It's time Liam and I move. My parents have retired to Florida, and while Liam feels responsible for Mason's dad, I'm sure we can convince him to move. Besides, Bianca could use a roommate or Harrison's mom.

6

KATELYN

As soon as I see Josie, all is right in the world. For as long as I can remember, she has been my rock, my go to... my best friend. Not seeing her every day is the drawback of living in California, but that's where my kids are. If I could be in two places at once, I would be. Because where Josie is, so is Mason

I thought about suggesting we meet in Beaumont for purely selfish reasons. I miss Mason's dad and would like to try my hand at convincing him to move closer to me. There was a time when I thought he and Harrison's mom would become more than friendly, but what I thought was happening was nothing more than two parents getting along for their children.

Harrison likes having him around as well. He was the same age as the twins when his father was killed and I think having Mason's dad around filled the void

Harrison felt. Mr. Powell is also very supportive of Quinn, giving him the chance to have a grandfather.

The other reason is Mason. Sometimes I feel like I'm betraying him by not being in Beaumont to tend to his grave. I know his father does it and so does Josie, but he was my husband and the father of my daughters. A part of me feels like I should always be there, but that wouldn't be fair to Harrison.

Josie returns from the bathroom and takes off her cover-up. I spit my drink out all over my lounge chair as she stands in front of Jenna and me with her hands on her hips.

"What in the..." I start to say, trying to contain my laughter at the bikini she has on. Only Liam would do something like this, to mark her so everyone knew she was taken. Not that she would ever look in another man's direction.

"You've got to be kidding me," Jenna says. "That is something Jimmy would do."

"Right! But no, my husband thought he'd be funny and had this waiting for me when I got off the plane."

Josie sits down with a huff. I half-expect her to cover up, but she doesn't. I know she's proud to wear the swimsuit. Our waitress appears with a fresh round of drinks and appetizers.

"This is paradise," Josie says as she sips her cocktail. After she sets it down, she reaches for my hand. "Are you okay?" she asks, knowing that my thoughts weigh heavily on my mind.

"Wait, what's going on?" Jenna asks, sitting up. I

look from her to Josie and back to Jenna, who moves over to my chaise lounge. "I knew something was bothering you earlier."

Taking a deep breath, I bite my lower lip to keep the tears at bay. "Today is the anniversary of when Mason proposed," I say, shaking my head. "I know it's just a day and that most people don't remember it twenty-plus years later, but I do. Each year, it's like a ton of bricks weigh heavily on my chest."

Josie slides over next to me and pulls me into her arms. "We're here for you."

"It's stupid, right?" I ask them. "I mean who's to say that Mason and I would even be married right now."

Both Jenna and Josie gasp. "You don't mean that, do you?" Jenna asks.

I shrug because I don't know. "When Harrison is gone and I'm lonely, my mind wonders. It plays the what-if game and I find myself asking the most ridiculous questions, ya know."

"Been there, done that," Josie says.

"Right, I mean what happens if Mason doesn't die? Does Liam still come home? Because if he doesn't, I don't meet Harrison and I can't imagine not having him in my life."

I turn away, angry with myself for bringing this up while we're supposed to be on vacation.

"I can't imagine my life being any different," Jenna says. "As much as I loved Mason, his death brought Jimmy to me, and Eden." Jenna reaches for my hand. "I don't want to sound selfish, but—"

"I get it, Jenna. You don't have to explain yourself because I'm there too, which makes me feel like a horrible person." I rest my head on Josie's shoulder.

"Tell me about your proposal," Jenna says in a bid to lighten the mood. Josie snorts and sits up, preparing for me to tell the story, even though Josie knows it well.

"Everything with Mason revolves around football, right? So, he calls me one day and tells me to meet him on the field. This is not out of the ordinary. He would often be there working out, running the snake and whatnot. So, I go out there and there are rose petals everywhere. The entire field is lined with rose petals and in the center of the field is Mason, dressed in a tuxedo that is too small for him.

"Of course, I make sure to step over each yard line so I don't mess up the roses as I walk to him. He doesn't even say anything. He just drops down onto his knee and asks me to marry him. I said yes. I mean he knew I would."

"Do you still have the ring?" Josie asks.

"I do. Gosh, remember how small it was?" I ask her. She nods.

"I used to think it was the biggest diamond ever, but God, we were so poor. I don't even know how he saved money to buy it."

"That's because love doesn't know size," Jenna says, and she's right. I look down at the ring on my finger now and smile.

"I've saved it for the girls. I know they probably won't use it, but it's there if they want it." Deep down, I know they'll never ask for it. Most of the time I wonder if the memories they have of Mason are theirs or just their imagination from the stories they've been told. They were five when he died, barely old enough to keep full-fledged memories. I hate that for them.

"One of them may surprise you," Josie says. But I doubt it. The girls have grown up in a lifestyle that doesn't equate to the way their father and I started out. I'm okay if they don't use it, but don't know what to do with it if they don't.

"This is dreary talk. We're supposed to be on vacation," I remind them. I sit up and the girls adjust. "How's Noah?"

"He's good. I think he's ready for the season to be over."

"Is he coming home?" I ask.

Josie shrugs. "I don't know. Maybe to visit, but there's Dessie..." she sighs. I've met Dessie and can understand why Josie feels the way she does. "Anyway, they have an apartment so I imagine he'll stay there."

"Do you think he'll ask her to marry him?" Jenna asks.

Josie covers her face with her hands. "I don't want to be that mom, but I hope not. I just don't like her and I've tried so hard to be open minded but she just doesn't fit in with us. She's not family orientated."

"Then this isn't the place for her," Jenna adds. She's right, we're family through and through. Aunts and uncles to each other's children.

"I have to find a way to like her," Josie mumbles.

She looks away briefly before turning her attention toward us. "What about Quinn?"

I smile proudly at the mention of my son's name. "He's doing his thing, playing in coffee shops, small gigs in the park. He's having fun and he loves that Elle is living there. They're talking about getting an apartment together when she finishes out the semester. She doesn't want to live on campus anymore."

"I'm surprised she didn't pledge?" Jenna wants to know.

"I know, me too. I thought she would, but her major keeps her out late at night and she didn't want the obligations that come with being in a sorority."

It was Josie's and my plan to pledge when we got to State, but that all changed rather quickly when Josie found out she was pregnant. At that point, Mason and I did everything we could to keep her in school. Liam already broke her heart. We didn't want her future ruined too.

"Peyton called the other day to talk to Liam. I tell ya he lights up like a Christmas tree when he hears her voice."

"What did she want?" I ask Josie. Not that it's any of my business, but I worry about her the most.

"To tell him that she was given some assignment or something. He kept telling her how proud he was of her."

"On Sunday, she's walking the sidelines for the Bears. Her teacher asked her if she would like to write up the recap of the story as part of her project," I tell them.

"You know before long, Peyton is going to be on television and we'll all sit around screaming that we know her," Jenna says, who in her own right has a daughter who's making a name for herself.

"And Ben?" Josie waggles her eyebrows and laughs. I shake my head. Benjamin is Elle's best friend, but that's it.

"Nothing. Elle brought him home last weekend. I looked for a sign, but there was nothing. I honestly think they're just friends."

"That's too bad. Ben's cute," Jenna adds. That he is with his baby-blue eyes and dark hair, but interested in him, my daughter is not.

I wipe away a few errant tears that have fallen and smile at my friends. I pull them both into a hug and hold them there briefly before letting them go. Josie, with her Liam-autographed swimsuit, goes back to her chaise and brings her umbrella drink to her lips, with Jenna doing the same.

"Hello, ladies." A man stands at the end of our cabana. Water drips down his chiseled body, disappearing into the waistband of his swim shorts. There isn't a drop of ink on his skin and I find myself wondering what Harrison would look like without his many tattoos. It's an image that I can't even imagine. My hand brushes against the flowers on my hip. It's my only tattoo. I've thought about getting more, but don't know what I'd get and honestly feel rather old.

49

"Hi, are you our waiter?" Josie asks. I have a feeling she knows that he's not. Jenna and I stifle a laugh.

"No, ma'am, but I'd like to buy you lovely ladies a few drinks," he says, rubbing his hand over his chest. Inside, I cringe, wondering if this is what my daughters go through when men try to pick them up. I can't even fathom Quinn acts like this.

"I think we're okay," Jenna says, shaking her drink in the air before taking a sip.

"Look, my buddies and I have a cabana over there." He points over his shoulder. "Why don't you ladies join us for a good time?"

As if on cue, we all raise our left hand and wiggle our fingers. Even though Harrison and I aren't officially married, we are common law, and even if we weren't, there isn't a man alive that could take me away from him.

Our lothario puts his hands up. "My apologies," he says. "Please tell your husbands they're very lucky."

As soon as he's out of earshot, I say, "Damn, that felt good."

"I can't wait to tell Jimmy that some guy hit on me," Jenna says, laughing.

"Yeah, I think I'll keep that one to myself," Josie adds.

"You know Liam will find out. If Jenna tells Jimmy, he'll blab like a little girl and tell Liam and Harrison."

Josie and I give Jenna a pointed look. She throws her hands up in the air and laughs. "Fine, I won't tell the Brit."

7

JENNA

The masseuse works the knots in my back like a magician. Her hands are soft, yet firm, but it's her fingers that are really doing the best job. Each push or jab into my skin gives me instant relief and dare I say it, satisfaction. I want to moan but I'm afraid I might frighten her. The last thing I want to do is make her feel uncomfortable, even though I'm the one naked and lubed up.

Thinking of myself like that has me in a fit of giggles. Jimmy would be all over this right now. Being a bass player, his fingers are nimble and can work some magic when my neck is sore, but this lady... well, I want to take her home with me.

"What has you laughing over there?" Josie mumbles. I turn my head and look at her. She has her eyes closed and seems to be as blissed out as I am.

"I was just thinking that Jimmy would jump at the opportunity to be a masseur."

"Just for you," Josie says. "Jimmy is smitten with you and Eden. I can't imagine him looking at another woman."

"I agree," Katelyn says.

My masseuse giggles but quickly tries to hide it. It makes me wonder if she's realized who we are. Josie and Katelyn laugh, quickly affirming my suspicions. On that note, I stop talking and go back to enjoying my massage. This isn't the place for us to discuss the men or what other jobs they'd like to have in their lives.

As soon as we're done, we find ourselves in the sauna. For right now, it's only the three of us and we can speak freely.

"Katelyn, do you wish you and Harrison had a child together?"

She smiles. "Yes and no. It's not like we were safe all the time. We went with the notion that if it happened, great. If not, we already had three amazing children. Now, we're at the stage where we could be grandparents soon."

"God, don't remind me," Josie adds. "Every time I see a magazine with Noah's face on it, I fear that the headline says something about him becoming a father."

"You're not ready?" I ask Josie.

"It's not that, it's... oh God, I am horrible. It's Dessie. I just can't find something to like about her, and I feel like the worst mother in the world."

Josie covers her face and her shoulders shake. Neither Katelyn nor I move to comfort her. It's like we both know she needs this moment to let it all out.

When she pulls her hands away, I'm unable to tell if she has shed any tears due to the moisture from the sauna.

"What don't you like about her?" Katelyn asks.

Josie shakes her head. "Liam said I don't like her because she's with Noah, but that's not it. She just acts like she owns him. Like he can't think for himself. When we were in Los Angeles for his game not too long ago, Elle went right up to him and hugged him, and Dessie stood there with her arms crossed looking really pissed."

"I remember," Katelyn says. "That night, Quinn was going on about how things used to be different between them."

"Eden likes her, but I think it's because she's a supermodel," I add. "You have to follow your instincts, right?"

Josie nods, as does Katelyn. "I'm trying to find common ground with her because I know she's important to Noah." Josie leans her head back against the tile wall. "This is like history repeating itself. Bianca hated me when Liam first brought me home. I remember I wasn't allowed in the house if she wasn't home, and she and Sterling made me feel miserable. Liam would sneak me over all the time. I don't want to be that version of Bianca."

"Eden talks about this surfer kid from Australia named Dane Foster all the time. I've met him a couple of times. He's cute. Has an accent. Dane's coming over to the house this week and will meet Jimmy for the first time. It's funny because he used to tease Eden about her crush on Quinn, but now that she really has one, he's freaking out."

"Those accents will get you every time," Katelyn says, laughing.

"Don't I know it."

"Why didn't you cancel her party?" Josie asks.

I adjust my towel and stretch my legs out. The tiles are cold against my heated skin. "I thought about it but Jimmy didn't want to interrupt her plans. He's having a hard time letting her grow up."

"That's easy to understand. I have a hard time with Quinn paying his own bills. I still want to mother him. The only thing he really allows me to do is his laundry."

The three of us laugh.

"Why didn't you and Jimmy have another baby?" Katelyn asks.

Josie and Katelyn both make eye contact with me. I smile and shake my head. "We tried. We did everything humanly possible but I just couldn't get pregnant. We thought about using a surrogate when Eden was about six or seven, but Jimmy and I both have trust issues and decided not to."

"I would've done it for you," Josie says.

"Me too. All you had to do was ask," Katelyn tells me.

I nod and try to hold back the tears, but to no avail. They pour out of me like a leaky faucet that can't shut off. The girls start to move toward me, but I hold my hand up "I'm okay. I read so many horror stories about surrogates and using friends that I didn't want to ruin our relationship."

"I think the bond we have is different from those stories you read. We were friends with you long before Liam brought the guys into our lives. It's a bonus that the three of us are best friends and married to the band, but that doesn't mean we still aren't your family."

"Katelyn's right, Jenna. I'm just sorry it's too late. I can't imagine being pregnant now. I'd probably park myself on the couch and eat Bon Bons all day and go back to watching the *Young and the Restless*."

I snort, laugh, and cough at the same time. "We're thinking about adopting, sort of. I've bought it up, but Jimmy is on the fence. Thing is, Eden's almost fifteen and I don't know if I want to do diapers or midnight feedings again."

"So, adopt a young child from another country," Katelyn suggests. "I'm always seeing those 'save the children' ads that are meant to make you cry, especially when you're already an emotional mess while watching TV."

"That might be easier than what Liam and I did," Josie says.

"You haven't spoken much about that time." I add.

She shakes her head and offers a quick smile. "It was hard, ya know. I had the room ready to go. I had heard his heartbeat and seen him on the monitor. She kept telling us that she didn't want him. She wouldn't even look at the screen during the ultrasound. Then

Aubrey calls one day and he's no longer mine, and I'm pregnant."

"Like it was meant to be," I say, but she shrugs.

"He's in Betty Paige's class so I see him all the time. I always wonder if he would smile more if Liam and I were his parents."

"Why do you say that?" Katelyn asks.

"His dad bailed when he was almost two and from what I hear around town, he doesn't pay child support. Meredith tries..."

"But it isn't the lifestyle you and Liam would've given him?" I ask.

Her lips go into a fine line as she nods. "I hate thinking about it because I have no doubt in my mind that Meredith loves him, but... I don't know. If I hadn't had Paige, I don't think I would've done it again. The heartache was too much even when I knew I was having my own. I missed the son I thought I was getting, but that doesn't mean it won't be right for you and Jimmy."

The mood seems to turn somber and I can't help but feel as if I caused this. "What do you say we go and get some ice cream?"

"Ice cream?" Katelyn looks confused at the notion.

I shrug. "It makes everything better, at least that's the line Eden uses on me when she's hurt, upset, or knows that she's done something wrong."

Josie laughs. "She gets that from Noah. This one time I had asked him to watch Paige while I ran to the store. He was glued to the television, watching some highlight show or whatever. It was my fault for not making sure he listened to me.

"When I came home, Noah had this big bowl of ice cream waiting for me. He handed it to me with a smile and went and unloaded the groceries from the car without asking. That was where he went wrong. When he came back in, I asked him where Paige was and the color drained from his face. He told me my mom was there and that they were upstairs. Turned out that Noah let Paige color... all over herself with a Sharpie. He panicked and called my mom to come help."

"Did he get in trouble?" Katelyn asks.

Josie nods and starts laughing. "After I finished the ice cream."

We leave the room laughing, but I still feel awkward after the adoption conversation. It's something I should bring up to Jimmy and see how he wants to proceed. Maybe Katelyn is right and we should look at adopting from another country. We could give a child a decent life here.

After quick showers, we're walking back toward our hotel when we come across a stand selling shaved ice. "It's my favorite," I say as I step up and order one. The girls quickly follow suit. "You know, I always want to do random jobs. I keep telling Jimmy that the next time they go on tour, I'm going to get a job working in a food truck or at the county fair."

I glance at Katelyn and Josie, they seem slack jawed at my confession. I shrug. "What?"

"Why would you want to work in a greasy, hot truck?" Josie asks as if the idea is disgusting.

"Why not? Think of the people you'd meet. Besides, I'm bored at home. Jimmy is always with Harrison, and Eden is in school." I take my shaved ice and thank the man. I start eating mine while Josie and Katelyn wait for theirs. "Katelyn, aren't you bored?"

She looks at me and smirks. "Yes, but that doesn't mean I'm going to join the carnival." She laughs.

"Why don't you apply at a florist?" Josie asks.

"Why don't you move to Cali and bring Whimsicality with you?" I counter.

She looks from me to Katelyn and shakes her head. "Our home is in Beaumont."

There's a bit of finality in her voice, the way she tells us that's where their home is. Sometimes I wonder if she's mad at us for leaving. With Harrison being from Los Angeles and Jimmy living there when he moved over from England, it made sense that they'd want to move back. Liam had only been there for ten years and Josie was established in Beaumont.

When they finally have their treats, I stick my very blue tongue out at them. It feels good to be a bit childish to lighten the mood.

8

JOSIE

It feels good to not have to worry about what people think of me or us as we continue to stick our tongues out at each other. Mine is red, Katelyn's is purple and Jenna's is blue. We giggle and join arms to walk along the path as a trio, a solid unit of friendship.

That's what we've been since Jenna arrived in Beaumont. She fit in right away, as if she had been a part of Katelyn and my life growing up. Jenna got our jokes, understood my plight with Liam, and was there when Mason died. She helped pick up the pieces and mold us all back together.

We reach our cabana, high on sugar and completely giddy. There are some guys swimming, and we ogle them. They did it to us yesterday, making us feel desired. Liam does that for me every day, sometimes multiple times, but there's some inner satisfaction knowing I can still turn the head of a nice-looking man.

From our cabana, we can see the sunset. Aside from the different coloring of the sky, one would never know it's night. The temperature hasn't changed. It feels as nice as it did when we walked out here this morning.

In the pool, I hear the name Noah yelled. I quickly scan the area, looking for my son even though I know there isn't any conceivable way that he would be here. It's football season and the Portland Pioneers mean more to him than anything. Well, almost anything. I hate thinking that Dessie could mean more, but that's where my mind is going.

I spot the couple, laughing and splashing each other. They seem happy and in love. But they're young. I remember when I was ridiculously in love with Liam, back in high school. That love was different from what we share now. It was all consuming. He's all I thought about from the time I woke until the time my brain rested. All day. Every day. I couldn't get enough of him, and in hindsight, that's why the breakup was so bad and one sided.

I was blinded by how I felt and couldn't see what was in front of me. The love of my life was struggling, and not just at home. He had made a heartfelt decision to attend a school that Mason had been accepted. It was a school that didn't need him and wouldn't for a few years, but they recruited him nonetheless. Liam was following his best friend, and that backfired.

And I pushed him to go back. If I could do it all over again, if I could open that door and hold him, and not encourage him to call the coach, I wonder how my life would've been different.

Would Liam have taken me with him to California? He says he would've, but I don't know. And what about Noah? If I could have told Liam I was pregnant that night, would he have stayed and raised our child, or would he have followed his heart that clearly led him to Los Angeles?

Over the years, I think about what his grand-mother was like, and why she had such a powerful pull on him. Did he tell her about me before she died? Did she know that I would've done anything to support Liam in his endeavors, even though I didn't come across that way to him? When we're eighteen, we think we know everything. But looking back, I didn't know shit. And I especially didn't know how to be a mother.

"What should we do for dinner?" Katelyn asks.

"I almost gave Noah up for adoption," I tell them, blurting it out like it's common knowledge I need to remind my friends. No one knows this, except for Mason. I never told Katelyn out of fear she would judge me for not wanting my child. It wasn't that I didn't want him. I was scared the closer I got in my pregnancy.

Telling my parents that I was pregnant was the hardest thing I had ever done. Not because I thought they would be disappointed in me, but I had to tell them that Liam was gone. The rage my father flew into will never be erased from my mind. He threatened to go over to the Westburys and demand to speak to Liam, but I promised him I would go instead.

I did, and it was horrible. Sterling answered the door and I told him I needed to get in touch with Liam, that it was urgent that I speak with him. I was crying, unable to keep my emotions in check. Sterling told me he was happy Liam finally got rid of the trash. I blurted out I was pregnant. *"The whore finally did it."* I will never, as long as I live, forget those words.

That was the time I thought about giving my child up for adoption. Deserted by its father and hated by its grandparents, everything felt hopeless.

When I told my mother my plan, she cried and asked me to be very sure of my decision. Thing is, I wasn't. Deep down, I wanted this child, the one Liam and I created; I knew it had been made from love.

I cried to my mother, who held me tightly against her chest, promising me that everything would be okay. My parents, as much as they hated the idea that I was eighteen and pregnant, wanted me to keep the baby.

When the school counselor suggested I consider adoption, I knew I never would. It wasn't for me. The baby growing inside of me was already loved.

"What?" Katelyn stammers. I keep my gaze on the young couple in the pool, mostly afraid to look at her. This is the one secret I've kept from her.

Taking a deep breath, I finally turn and glance at my two best friends. Tears well in my eyes and I cover them out of shame. Their arms are wrapped around me instantly. I don't deserve their love, not right now.

"I thought it would be best for the baby if they didn't grow up in Beaumont. I didn't know what Sterling and Bianca would do when they saw me with the child out and about, and feared they would try to harm or take the baby away from me. I figured adoption would be best."

"Did Mason know?" Katelyn asks. I nod my head. "I thought so," she says. Katelyn clears her throat, and I turn to look at her.

"Mason went to Los Angeles to look for Liam," I tell her.

"How did you know?" Katelyn asks.

I clear my throat, and try to smile. "It was in Sam's journal. She talked about Mason waiting for Liam to show up. She also made sure Liam never got my phone message."

"That woman was vile," Jenna says.

I laugh. "You don't know the half of it. We can't prove it, but Liam and I are pretty sure she paid Alicia to drug Harrison."

"Quinn's mom?" Jenna asks.

"Biological mother," Katelyn corrects her. "I'm his mother." Katelyn is never one to shy away when asked if Quinn is her son, but bring up Alicia and she changes her tune. "That woman... I swear."

"She's as bad as Sam was," I say. "Sometimes I wonder if they aren't related. I still feel like Sam is lurking around the corner."

"Jimmy's ex, Chelsea. She calls every now and again," Jenna says, shrugging.

"Are her and his father still together?" I ask.

Jenna shakes her head. "Nope. Left her high and dry with the baby. She calls, looking for James, thinking that Jimmy knows where he is, but he doesn't. He hasn't spoken to his dad since he was in the hospital. Chelsea's tried to get Jimmy to be a big brother to her son. She wants Eden to hang out with him. Jimmy refuses though."

"You seem... pensive?" Katelyn suggests.

"I feel sorry for the boy, ya know? He didn't ask for his dad to be like this, and I think Jimmy is a bit harsh, but I get it." She shrugs. "His ex had an affair with his dad and tried to pin it on him. That shit messes people up."

"She tried to break you guys up," I point out.

"Hey, I said nothing about Chelsea hanging out, just the boy," she laughs.

"Have you seen him?" Katelyn asks.

"Yeah, he looks just like Jimmy. For a while, I thought Jimmy was his dad. I asked for a DNA test. Jimmy took one and it showed that they're related, but that Jimmy wasn't his father."

"Jesus, have you ever looked at our lives and asked how it is that we're so normal when everything around us is fucking crazy? We're like our own reality show," I say.

"But with low ratings and no viewers," Katelyn adds.

The three of us start laughing. We're loud and

slightly obnoxious. I pull my best friends into a hug, thankful that I have them in my life.

"For what it's worth," Katelyn says. "I'm happy you didn't give Noah up for adoption."

"Me too," Jenna adds.

"Me three," I state. "That boy was the light of my life. He's my one piece of Liam that I got to hang onto. It's funny, by the time I gave birth, I was healed. I had Mason and you." I bump shoulders with Katelyn. "My parents. I was happy."

"Where does Nick come in?" Jenna asks.

I sigh. "Nick was just there. He treated Noah for a cold or something and we just kept talking after that."

"I remember in high school that Nick was so smart."

"Too smart for his own good," I say. "The man fast tracked through college and medical school. Who the hell can do that?"

"Apparently Nick," Jenna says.

"Aubrey's good for him though, and Amelie is the cutest little girl."

"And Mack?" Katelyn asks, knowing full well that he's a sore subject.

"And Mack is handsome, like his father. Sweet like his mother."

"And fancies your daughter?" Jenna adds.

I nod. "Liam's going to kill him."

"What do you say we go get dinner like you suggested?" I lean into Katelyn. "Then after dinner and a few drinks, we'll call the guys."

"Better yet, we should Facetime them," Jenna says.

"Yeah, that sounds fun, as long as we're all in the same bed."

"Josie, you really know how to turn my husband on." Jenna laughs as we all link arms and head toward the hotel.

9

KATELYN

Our week is half over and it feels like we just got here. It could be because all we do is sit around and gossip, or reminisce about our past, and think aloud about what the future might hold for us. Thing is, we could've done this in Beaumont or Los Angeles and saved ourselves a ton of money. Don't get me wrong, being in paradise is great. Being doted on by staff has its perks, but I miss home.

I miss Harrison. I miss the kids. I miss my condo on the beach that has become my home.

As I stare out into the ocean, the surfers all settle and wait for the next wave to ride in. Harrison taught the girls to surf, and I remember their first time out in the waves I was so scared. Even though I had watched Quinn do it many times, something about the girls being out there freaked me out.

But they conquered. Peyton and Elle learned to ride the waves, right along with Harrison and Quinn.

It's hard to put a finger on what the girls have taught Harrison. When he came into our lives, he had everything, except for a wife, and he didn't need that. I had a hard time fathoming why a man would want a widow with two small children.

I asked him once and his reply was, "Why wouldn't I?"

My phone rings, tearing my eyes away from the surfers. The picture I use of Quinn shows on the display on my phone.

"Hello?"

"Hey, Mom," he says. Just hearing him makes my day brighter. "Are you having fun?"

"I am, sort of. I miss you guys. I've been thinking we need a family vacation."

"That'd be fun. Maybe we should go skiing around Christmas?"

"Oh yes, that would be lovely, although Peyton may want to go somewhere warm."

Quinn laughs because he knows I'm right. "Probably. We'll compromise and do two weeks. One in Vail and the other wherever she wants to go."

Before Harrison and I took the plunge and became a couple, I had heard horror stories about merging two families. I had nightmares about the girls not getting along with Quinn or him tormenting the girls. The thought that they'd grow up hating each other was enough to make me sick. Thankfully, the kids proved the statistics wrong.

"That sounds like a plan. So, what are you up to today?"

"Nothing much. I'm thinking about driving down to see Dad, maybe take the boards out."

"That's what I'm doing now, watching the surfers. I think you guys would love it down here."

"Did you go on the big water slide?"

I start to laugh. "No, that's today. I'm just waiting for your aunts to be ready to go. I think we're swimming with the dolphins too. Your dad and uncles certainly spared no expense making sure we were well taken care of."

"Did you expect anything different?"

My head shakes, even though he can't see me. "Honestly, no. But I was under the impression this was supposed to be a low-key affair. I don't know if Josie and Katelyn know this or not, but we have a bodyguard. He hangs in the shadows but he's there, watching."

"Lurking," he adds.

"Quinn, you know it's for protection."

When the kids were little and word got out that the band was living in Beaumont, the paparazzi were sometimes relentless. They weren't always around unless the guys had a new album coming out or they were on tour and reporting some ridiculous scandal. The guys didn't take too kindly to the kids being followed, and hired bodyguards. It was for their protection, but when you're a teenager and trying to date, having someone watching your back can be a bit unwelcoming.

"I know, but doesn't mean I had to like it. Anyway,

I wanted to check to see how your trip was going and thought you'd want to come up when you get home and check out my new set? I have a few new gigs lined up. One is at this pretty happening coffee shop."

"You know I'll be there, Quinn."

"I love you, Mom." He hangs up before I can return the sentiment. Deep down, I know he knows that I love him, but I like telling him. When he was younger, he liked to hear it. I think it was reaffirming for him to know that he was loved, especially with how Alicia had treated him and his dad.

I've never understood how a mother could do that, especially to someone like Quinn. Although, had she met him, I fear we would've been entangled in a war over custody, visitation, and money. For the longest time, that's what I thought she wanted, but Harrison told me she never asked for a dime. The day she showed up at his apartment with Quinn in his carrier, she just left them there. Every day, I thank God she didn't want to be a mother to that boy because I did, and I have cherished every moment since he was brought into my life.

Now that I've spoken with Quinn, I press the number for Peyton. I know she'll be awake and more willing to talk. Unlike her sister, Peyton doesn't stay up partying all night. Elle tells me it is part of her degree that she needs to be on the scene looking for talent. Harrison and Quinn agree with her, while I call bullshit. But what the hell do I know? I'm only the mother.

"Hey, Mama," Peyton says as she answers the

phone. "Please tell me it's freezing cold down there because that's the only thing that is going to get me through today."

"You'll be fine. They have those giant heaters on the field. If you get cold, stand by one."

"I think those are for the players," she tells me.

"Feign innocence. Bat your eyelashes at the security guard. Ooh, better yet, flirt with one of the players and maybe he'll give you one of those super big jackets that we always see Noah wearing."

Peyton laughs loudly. "I'm not doing that, Mom. I'll be sure to bundle up."

Elle would. That's the difference between the two girls. Elle won't think twice about using her sexuality to get what she wants. It's bothersome, but seems to be the norm in Hollywood. Harrison tells me all the time that Elle has strong morals and just because she's flirting doesn't mean she's selling herself out.

Peyton, on the other hand, is reserved, but knows when to turn on the charm. She doesn't overdo it often; she prefers the background over the limelight. Not sure how that is going to work for her since she wants to be behind the desk on national television.

"Do you think I'll be able to see you on TV today?"

"Probably not. The cameras focus mostly on the players and coaches. No one really cares about the sideline reporters."

"Well I do, and so does everyone else you know."

"Noah says that I have to stand way in the back, behind the boom mic so that I don't get run over."

"Wait, is there a chance you'll get trampled?" I ask, now worried that she might get hurt.

"I doubt it. It's not like in high school when I could have my toe on the sideline. I'll be on the field, but during game play, media is required to stand in one spot."

"Phew, okay. Oh hey, I was talking to Quinn a few minutes ago and I've decided that we need a vacation. He wants to ski—"

"Ugh, I live in Chicago and it's snowing."

"And he suggests we go somewhere warm for a week. Wherever you want to go."

"Yes! That is what I'm talking about. A week sitting by the fire place in a lodge while my overly sun-kissed family skis and a week basking in the sun while you guys stay inside with the AC."

It takes me a minute to realize that she's being sarcastic. I sigh heavily, knowing there isn't any way to appease everyone.

"Well, if you have another suggestion, your father and I would be happy to hear it."

"It's just..."

I know what she's going to say, but she refuses to finish her sentence. If Elle and she had gone to school together, things would be different. Peyton wanted them to be at the same school, while Elle wanted something completely different. It's not unheard of with twins.

"We'll work it out when I get home. Maybe we'll invite everyone."

"The days of all of us taking family vacations are long gone. Noah's too busy."

"I suppose you're right. The days of big family vacations are long past us."

"Yep, sucks," she says. "Okay, I should probably go and read my notes on the players. I don't want to get caught not knowing my stuff."

"That would never happen. I'm so proud of you, Peyton."

"Thanks, Mom. Love you."

"Love you too, baby girl."

Once we hang up, I'm back to staring at the surfers. A few wipe out, causing me to laugh. Every time Harrison falls off his board, he tells me it was planned and that he needs to do that every now and again to psyche himself out. I let him think that I believe him and tell him that he crashed gracefully.

I decide to call Elle, not caring whether I wake her up or not. She answers on the fifth ring, gasping for air. I close my eyes and try to block out any imagine that pops into my mind about why she can't breathe.

"Aren't you on vacation?" she asks.

"Hello, my darling daughter. How are you?"

"Hi, Mom. Busy."

"Did I catch you at a bad time?"

"No. Maybe. I'm trying to get dressed before Quinn gets here. He called and begged me to head down with him today."

My heart soars, filling with love. "Oh, okay. Well, I

had spoken to your brother and sister today and didn't want you to feel left out."

"No worries, Mom. Quinn filled me in. Family vacation. Two weeks. One warm. One cold. Got it. Quinn's here, gotta go. Love you."

I pull my phone away from my ear and watch the call go dead. She is so opposite from Peyton, but used to be her shadow. It wasn't until college that she developed this new sense of freedom. I know she doesn't always need me, but dammit, I'm her mother and I need her sometimes.

Instead of calling Harrison, I send him a text. I don't know if he's already surfing or what. For all I know, he's playing the drums and won't answer anyway.

Take care of my babies. Don't forget Peyton's game is on.

You forget they're my babies too. I love you, Katelyn. Everything will be fine.

Enjoy your time with your friends.

Noah's game is on too. We'll be watching both.

I love you

I know he won't text back because he doesn't want to take away from this trip. He knows how important it is for Josie, Jenna, and me to get away and not worry about what's happening back home. What he doesn't understand is that back home is where I'd rather be. It's not that I don't like being here; it's just that I want everyone together.

10

JENNA

"Mum, everything is a disaster!" Eden screeches into the phone. I pull it away from my ear to quell the ringing. "Mummy, are you there? I think we should call Grandma and ask her to come out here until you're home. Daddy is telling me he's going to show Dane his gun collection."

Remember that vacation Jimmy said I needed so badly and I didn't want to take? This is why—they fight and he does something to piss Eden off. She in turn has a teenage drama fit, which just makes the situation worse, like now.

"Eden, your father doesn't own a gun, let alone have a collection of them," I tell her as I toss my head back in frustration. One week. They only had to find common ground for one week.

"He says he does, along with Uncle Liam and

Harrison. He said he's calling in the Arsenal. I don't even know what gang that is!"

And that right there is the drawback of living in California. She thinks a football team is a gang. "Oh Eden, Arsenal are a football team that play in England. You and your dad went to some games one time when you were visiting your nana."

"Oh," she says, her once crazy, high-pitched voice is now back to normal.

"Here's the thing, Little One. Your father doesn't like the fact that you're growing up, okay? He's having a hard time with his baby girl not needing him, and the boy thing—every parent goes through this. Your Aunt Josie did the same with the girls that came around to date Noah, and I can bet you that Uncle Liam is about to go through this with Betty Paige."

"But it's not fair. I don't understand why he wants to harm Dane?"

"He doesn't, Eden. He wants to scare him. He wants that boy to know that if he hurts you, makes you cry, harms a single hair on your head, he will pay for it. Every dad who loves his little girl does this. It's a part of life."

"But, Mum..."

"No buts, and I'm not calling Grandma to come save you. You and your father need to learn how to coexist when I'm not there. Where is your dad?"

"Downstairs," she says, completely defeated.

"Let me talk to him."

"Um... he doesn't know I called you."

"Well, he will now. Put him on."

I hear her say, "Ugh!" but she has the phone pulled away so I can't really chastise her for her behavior.

"Sweet Lips?"

"Hey," I say with a sigh. It's so good to hear his voice. I would've felt the same about Eden calling if she didn't start off with an instant rant about her father.

"Why are you calling? You're supposed to be getting a tan, getting drunk, and flirting with every single man out there."

"Just the single men?" I ask.

"Well, yeah. I don't want any missus drama from some bloke's wifey." He laughs so hard that he starts choking.

"Jimmy... I can't even with you sometimes."

"But you love me."

"That I do, which is why we're talking. Please stop with the gun talk. You know I don't like it and Eden thinks Arsenal are some gang in California that are coming to shoot Dane."

"Good. It's better that way."

"Maybe it is, but not when I'm thousands of miles away and can't run interference. Be good to her, Jimmy. She's our baby."

"That's my point. This bloke is sniffing around and getting all hands-on with her, touching her on her back during her surf lessons. I don't like him, Jenna."

"Well, my father didn't like you much to start with either, remember?" When my father found out I was pregnant and married to Jimmy, he tried to buy him off, thinking that it would just be better for him to go away. I almost stopped speaking to my father after that. He never took my feelings into consideration. Granted, my earlier relationship didn't exactly work out the best and he was trying to protect me.

"You're hurting my pride, Sweet Lips. How am I supposed to be the man of the house if I can't make it known I'm the man of the house, when we have this guy sniffing around our baby girl? He needs to know his boundaries."

"You will be able to, if they start dating, but until that happens, let them flirt, Jimmy. They're never alone so there's no harm."

He sighs and I know from experience that he's running his hand through his hair. "All right, all right. You're right, wifey."

"I love you," I tell him. "I miss you like crazy."

"Just so you know, we're shagging in the car when you land. Be prepared."

"As if I would expect anything less."

We hang up shortly after that with him promising to make things better between Eden and him. I know he means well, but he still harbors a lot of resentment toward his father and doesn't know how to always act around Eden. Still, I want him to be a diligent father because the last thing I want is for her to end up in trouble.

I come out of my room to find Katelyn on the balcony talking on the phone. A quick search and I find Josie talking to Liam in her room. Who comes to paradise and spends most of the morning in their room? The wives of 4225 West, that's who. We're homesick, we get it, but damn we needed the time away. It's good for the men to be the moms for a bit. Lord knows we do the dad part more often than not.

Not that I nor Katelyn nor Josie blame the guys for not being home. We knew that going in; well, at least Katelyn and I did. Josie, on the other hand, was thrown into it, sink or swim. For the most part, she's held her head above water easily, except for the bullshit that Sam put her through with her from the grave journal.

For a while, Jimmy and I thought that Liam and Josie were going to split. Not that I shared my concerns with Josie. I don't know about Jimmy though. He lacks a filter sometimes and blurts out the most obscene things at the most inopportune time. But, Josie stood by her man, despite stupid tabloid rumors of another child and the diary from hell being published.

I know that someday, I'll be in her shoes. I'm waiting for Chelsea to publish her tell-all or for some random fan to hack into Jimmy's Twitter feed and exploit the gaggle of tweets he still gets to this day. Some just don't care that he's married and has a daughter. And maybe I get it. Celebrity crushes and all, but some of the tweets are downright crude and unacceptable.

As we make our way through the lobby, the staff members greet us. They're a bit loud and boisterous with their cheery hellos, drawing attention from the others who linger. We smile and continue on our way and into the lounge where we've requested Noah's game, along with the one Peyton is working at, be broadcast.

When we enter, the bartender changes it from soccer, aka football, to American football, causing the patrons to groan. The bartender shrugs and points to us, which doesn't make the situation any better. Three women needing to watch a sporting event is one of two things, either the highlight of a man's day, or the bane of his existence.

Aside from Noah's games, Jimmy spends most of his time watching rugby or surfing competitions with Eden. Recently, he's been watching American Ninja Warrior with hopes of trying out. My skinny British man who still suffers the effects from being shot wants to try out for the show. He's taken his quest to Xander, who has been trying to implement the routines into his gym. I wish my husband the best of luck.

Noah's face is shown on the big screen and Josie lights up. "That's my boy," she screams loudly. This, of course, gets everyone's attention, especially the men. A few come over to us and take the extra chairs surrounding our table. Only they don't talk to us, they turn and face the big screen. Katelyn and I make faces at them and each other, wondering what the hell they're doing.

"Does he look skinny to you?" Josie asks, her voice full of worry. Her head tilts side to side as she tries to take in every aspect of Noah's face while he's interviewed.

"He's on TV, you can't really tell," Katelyn says.

"She's not feeding him. All they do is eat out. I bet he hasn't had a home-cooked meal since the last time he was home."

"He's fine, Josie. Noah knows how to take care of himself," I say, but she shakes her head.

"Do you know that kid?" one of the men in front asks. I'm ready to ignore him and his friend for their rude behavior, but Josie isn't.

"That's my son," she says proudly.

"Wait, so you're the wife of that Liam guy my wife is constantly raving about?"

Josie nods, but her eyes are completely focused on the television screen. I glance at Katelyn who eyes them suspiciously. I've been around the industry long enough to know when something doesn't feel right, it usually isn't.

He finally turns around, but not before I see him pull out his cell phone. I let out a huge aggravated sigh. I'm irritated they've invited themselves to sit with us and our security guard isn't around to remove them. Maybe he's watching these guys and waiting for any sign of trouble. Of course, if we knew his name or had his number, we could text him and tell him to come and remove these two buffoons.

Josie's lost in her own little world with the Portland Pioneers on the field that she doesn't even notice the group of women that walk in, followed by a few more husbands. Before either Katelyn or I can say anything, they've surrounded themselves at our table, pulling every available chair over they can find.

I open my mouth to say something just as one of the women scoots in next to me and snaps a picture of us.

"Oh no, this one isn't any good. Let's do it again," she says. Unfortunately, I oblige because the last thing I want is for the guys to receive any bad press. "You're so lucky."

"Is that so?" I ask, taking a long drink off my cocktail. I signal to the bartender that I need another. It's going to be a long-ass day if I must be super nice.

"Jimmy's so hot."

Of course, that's why I'm lucky. Not because he's an amazing man but because he's hot. I should tell her he's excellent in bed and has a big dick to curb any notions she might have about asking me the finer details of my marriage.

I nod in agreement. "Thanks."

"RUN!" Josie scares the shit out of me when she yells at the television. I turn my attention there to see Noah running down the center of the field with many guys chasing after him. He slides before he can get tackled.

"Oh. My. God. You're Liam Page's wife. Like, holy shit," another woman says. "We love the Pioneers and Noah. We root for him all the time."

"Thanks," Josie says without making eye contact with them.

I look at Katelyn, who rolls her eyes. We have a decision to make. Do we let them stay and hang out, and give them the glory? For any fan, going back to your friends with the story that you hung out with the wives of 4225 West is something that can make a trip memorable.

But at who's expense? Not Josie's—she's focused on Noah, and it won't be Katelyn because she'll be watching the Bears game for any sign of Peyton. So, it comes down to me. I down the rest of my drink and make a mental note to tell Liam his bodyguard sucks because the Chatty Kathy next to me won't shut up about how great he is.

Man, if they only knew.

11

JOSIE

atching Noah's game, no matter where I am, is important to me. In hindsight, I should've asked that the bar be shut down for a private event, but I don't like using my husband's name to get what I want.

Katelyn and Jenna are being saints, even though I know they're pissed off. I am too, but at this moment, I don't care. My son is on television and the game is close. Noah's team isn't great, and he tells me it's because it's an expansion team that must build. He wants to carry that load though and shoulders each loss as if they're his fault. Liam, Nick, and I have both told him that he can't make the receivers hold onto the ball once they're tackled. That's their job. There is only so much a quarterback can do. Of course, when you're facing the likes of Tom Brady, I'm sure anyone feels inferior.

As his mother, I want him to win. I think it's what all mothers want. We want to see our children happy and proud of their accomplishments. In high school, he had that. Not always in football, but in baseball. So, when he chose the former as a career, I thought he was crazy. But I supported him. Encouraged him to be the best. And he is.

With every throw, my jaw is clenched. I'm waiting with baited breath to see if he's sacked, afraid that he'll take off running with the ball only to end up tackled or thrown and an errant pass that lands into the opposing team's hands, and when the ball does land where it's supposed to be, my heart starts beating again and everyone in the bar cheers the Pioneers on.

At halftime, I get up and stretch. I think about leaving, but the camera pans to Liam, Betty Paige, and Bianca. Paige has her nose stuffed into a book. Liam is focused on the field, probably the cheerleaders if I had to guess, and Bianca is talking to one of the people behind her. I find myself waving, only to realize that they can't see me. I miss them, even Bianca. Over the years, the dynamic of our relationship has changed for the better. She's very attentive to Noah and Paige, and has asked if Paige would like to come to California for the summer. She wants to try her hand at acting and with the connections that Grandma Betty had and with Bianca dabbling back into the business, Paige would have a fair shot at learning from some of the best.

The best thing Bianca ever did was leave Sterling.

He left Beaumont not long after their divorce was final. We thought Bianca would come back, but she sold the home she shared with him and Liam, which broke his heart a little bit. I understood where Liam was coming from with that, even though I have very few happy memories there. I hated sneaking around and always living in fear that I would be caught in his bedroom. At least at my house, Liam was welcomed, although not in my bedroom. Yet, we all know I didn't follow rules very well.

When you're a teenager, you break rules. I broke each one ever set up about Liam. If I hadn't, Noah wouldn't be here right now. I can't be sorry for not listening to my parents. However, I'll be damned sure that Betty Paige is more careful. I plan to talk to her about sex, and make sure that Nick and Aubrey do the same thing with Mack. I see the way they look at each other. I'm not stupid. I look at Liam the same way, always have.

"Hey, can I place an order for some food?" I ask the bartender.

"Of course, do you know what you'd like?"

"No," I say, shaking my head. "Why don't you give us two of each of the appetizers? There's a lot to feed and make sure their tabs are covered." I nod toward my table. I estimate about fifteen people sitting at or near my table.

I get the stardom thing. I used to have stars in my eyes when Liam first came back. The racing heart, the sweaty palms, and stuttering speech wasn't because I was in love with him, it was because he's Liam Page, sexy rock star god who has women dropping their panties with one look. I should know because I was one of them.

The night we rekindled it all was the night I asked him to be Liam Page when he took me out. I wanted to experience what others had in my place. But what I got was my Liam with a look I can only describe as smoldering. He had this presence about him, like he was in charge of the universe and it would sway on its axis any way he wanted. He treated me like a queen that night and I knew I wasn't getting Liam Page the rock star, but Liam Page the man who has loved me since I was fifteen.

I make my way back to the table and pull Jenna into a hug. "Thank you for being strong and dealing with these people. I owe you." And I'll pay her back, somehow.

"I know how important the games are to you," she says, squeezing me tighter.

I do the same for Katelyn, but say, "I love you."

"I love you too," she replies. When I pull away, she looks at me questioningly. I shake my head and turn toward the television just as our food arrives. The people who have commandeered our table have wide eyes and hungry stomachs.

"Dig in," I tell them. I can feel all eyes on me, trying to decipher if they heard me correctly. I nod and hands go flying toward the food. Katelyn and Jenna pull our favorites toward us, making sure that we have want we want.

"You're a saint," Katelyn tells me. I don't think of it like that, but see it as me doing a good deed. The people here may not ever get another chance like this, so why not make it worth something. They'll go home, post about it on their social media accounts, and it will be something happy for them. That's what I find to be important.

During halftime, the broadcast flips to other games. When Chicago comes on, the three of us are focused on the screen, scanning the sidelines for any sight of Peyton. Every day I wish she were two years older so she and Noah could be together. I know that's not what either of them wants but a mother can wish. I love the twins as if they were my own daughters, and Peyton has grown into such a well-rounded young woman. I think that is partly why I don't care for Dessie but know I need to find a way to accept her because I fear she's not going anywhere.

When halftime is over, the bartender turns the volume back up on the TV. And when Noah comes out, the entire place erupts in cheers. I can't help but smile for my boy and wish I was in that stadium with him right now.

As the game goes on, I grow more worried they're going to lose. That is until Noah throws a bomb of a pass for a touchdown. My hands are clasped together until I see us cross the goal line. I stand up and raise my arms, and start high-fiving everyone around me until I see the yellow flag on the field.

"What the fuck!" I say, much to the surprise of everyone around me. When the official shows the signal for holding, I let it all out. "That's fucking bull-shit," I yell at the TV.

"Yeah, it was," the guy in front of me says. Even as the play is shown again, it's clear that there wasn't a hold.

"Assholes."

Everyone around me starts laughing. I do too, although it's not funny. However, as Noah will tell anyone who listens, his mother cusses like a sailor when it comes to football.

I think the game is moving at a snail's pace, only it isn't. It's the two-minute warning and we're down by seven. Each play is more intense than the last as Noah marches them down the field. Everyone is tired and the linemen are getting closer to tackling my son. I need to be at the game, to tell his line to stay strong and protect their quarterback.

Noah takes center. He's mic'd so everyone can hear his cadence. He drops back and fires a torpedo of a pass into the arms of his friend, Chase Montgomery's, hands. I gasp loudly when a massive man tosses Noah to the ground, but my son picks his head up and watches the ball soar through the air, landing in Chase's arms and he runs it in for a touchdown.

"They gotta go for two," I say, only to have one of the men at the table disagree with me.

"No way, go for one. Tie it up."

I point at the screen. "Are you shitting me right now? There's too much time on the clock to just tie it up. Go for two and pray that our defense can hold them."

"She's right," his friend says. I look at him smugly and wish I could stick my tongue out at him. Sadly, I must be an adult and refrain from such childish behavior.

The Pioneers end up going for two, but in the end, it's not enough. I'm sad, but it's been par for the course this year. I order us all another round, knowing that I need it. Katelyn consoles me, which is ridiculous. Noah is the one who needs to be consoled, although he'd tell me things will get better. Sometimes I want to scream "when" because this mom is tired of them losing all the freaking time.

It's about an hour after the game when Liam calls. I honestly didn't expect him to call at all, but I'm glad to hear his voice.

"Hey, babe."

"Are you with Katelyn?" he asks.

"I am. Why, do you need to speak with her?"

"No, I need you to excuse yourself so we can speak in private." Liam's tone has me worried so I tell everyone that I'll be right back.

"What's going on? You're scaring me."

"Fuck, Josie... the plane is on its way to get you. You

need to get Katelyn on the plane immediately. If you don't have time to pack, I'll make sure housekeeping does it, but get to the airfield now."

"Liam?" My voice is shaky. I know something is wrong.

"It's Peyton, Jojo. She was in an accident and Harrison says it's not good."

"Oh, my God," I say, covering my mouth as tears steam down my face.

"He's been trying to reach her, but she isn't answering. He's freaking out. I'm on my way to Chicago now. I'll meet you there."

"Okay," I say as he hangs up.

My steps are wobbly as I make my way back to the table. Katelyn and Jenna see my face and immediately come rushing toward me. I take both their hands and lead them to the elevator.

"What's happening?"

"What's wrong?"

"Is it Noah?"

"Is it Paige?"

Those are the questions they keep asking until we've reached our room. Once inside, I break down. I take Katelyn's hands in mine and hold them tightly. "We gotta go, okay? The plane is going to be waiting for us so we need to pack as fast as we can and get to the airfield."

"Who is it?" she asks.

"It's Peyton."

There has been only one other time I have seen

Katelyn void of any color and that's when Mason died. I've prayed every day since that I would never see her like this again.

CONTINUE onto the sneak peek of HOLDING ONTO FOREVER ~ Releasing October 12th

ACKNOWLEDGMENTS

This book is purely for the fans who asked to hear from the wives!

Thank you for your continued support.

It's good to be back in Beaumont.

ABOUT THE AUTHOR

Heidi is a New York Times and USA Today Best-selling author.

Originally from the Pacific Northwest, she now lives in picturesque Vermont, with her husband and two daughters. Also renting space in their home is an over-hyper Beagle/Jack Russell, Buttercup and a Highland West/Mini Schnauzer, JiLL and her brother, Racicot.

When she's isn't writing one of the many stories planned for release, you'll find her sitting court-side during either daughter's basketball games.

Forever My Girl, is set to release in theaters on January 26, 2018, starring Alex Roe and Jessica Rothe.

Don't miss more books by Heidi McLaughlin! Sign up for her newsletter, follow her on Amazon, Book Bub or join the fun in her fan group!

Connect with Heidi!
www.heidimclaughlin.com
heidi@heidimclaughlin.com

SNEAK PEEK: HOLDING ONTO FOREVER

BY HEIDI MCLAUGHLIN

Noah

The crowd is deafening as I take the field. I don't need to look up at the scoreboard to know that there is under two minutes left and we're down by seven. Of course, if our last touchdown hadn't been called back for a bullshit call, we'd be tied, although, my mindset wouldn't be much different. This is our hurry-up offense that we practice the most. Some teams are better at it then we are, but we're young and still building the expansion team. Truth be told, no one expects us to win, and when we do, the sports analyst have a field day, jumping on the temporary bandwagon of the Portland Pioneers.

I'm used to the haters and have had to live with them badmouthing my dad for the past fifteen years. Being Liam Page's son hasn't been easy. Despite what critics say, everything that I have done, every achievement has been earned. My father was adamant that I make my own path, determine my own future. He didn't want me doing something I didn't want to do.

There was a time when I thought baseball was going to be my calling. My coach and somewhat stepdad, Nick, was convinced as well. After we won three consecutive state titles behind my pitching, the colleges were ready for me to commit to them and Major League teams were ready for me to sign my life away on the dotted line.

When I sat my parents down, which included Nick and Aubrey, I told them that I wanted to play football even though our high school team never made it past the first round of playoffs and the colleges weren't scouting me. I had a few small offers, but nothing that stood out. My parents supported my decision and were the ones to drive me to Notre Dame weeks before school started so I could walk on. It was the best decision I had ever made because within six games I was the starting quarterback and once the season was over I was offered a full-ride in exchange for three years of playing football with them.

After my junior year, I was encouraged by money hungry agents to enter the draft. My coach knew this was happening but never said anything. He didn't have to. I could see everything he was feeling in his expression. He was sad and worried that his star quarterback was ditching out a year early. It's not unheard of for an athlete to leave school early, but that wasn't for me. I made a commitment to the school that took a chance on me and really wanted to lead them to a bowl game. I did, but we didn't win. Still, it was one of the best decisions of my life.

And now here I am in my fourth year in the National Football League and the starting quarterback of a team that just wants to win. We have the tools in the players that we have. Our coach, Bud Walter, is one of the best but isn't here for the long haul. He's had a storied career and will be retiring soon, but until then he demands one hundred percent from us each and every time, and we do everything that we can to give it to him.

I stand behind the center Alex Moore. He's one of my best friends, not because he's meant to try and protect my ass from getting tackled or sacked each play, but because he's a stand-up guy who doesn't give a shit that my father is famous. I yell out my cadence and tap Alex on his ass in the event that he can't hear me. Once the pigskin touches my hands, I'm backpedaling with my arm cocked and ready to fire. My targets are the wide receiver, Julius Cunningham, who has been in the league for five years or Chase Montgomery the tight end. Chase is one of the best in the league and asked for a trade once the expansion team was announced. He's from Portland and wanted to be at home so his ailing mother could come to his games.

A monster of a tackle comes rushing toward me as I release the ball. I'm hit and thrown to the ground before I can see if it lands in Chase's hands. By the roar of the crowd, it does and I scramble to stand so I can get back to the line of scrimmage only to find Chase dancing in the end zone.

Coach yells that we go for two and I'm contemplating his thought process as I hurry toward my offensive line. Going for two means our opponent has to score. Tying the game means we can go a few more minutes. I have never second-guessed Bud, and I shouldn't be trying to now. I call out the play and resume my spot behind Alex. Once again my cadence is repeated and the ball is put into play.

The field before me is clear and I fire a rocket of a pass to Julius who catches it flawlessly in the end zone. My arms go up as I run toward him to celebrate, which is cut short because now we have to go back on defense.

"Westbury," Bud yells my name as I reach the sideline.

"Yeah, Coach?"

"Next time run more time off the clock."

I nod and walk toward the bench and sit down. He's right. I should've run some small routes instead of opening it up for the deep pass. Now we have to hold them on defense. I have faith in our cornerback, Cameron Simmons, but he can't cover everyone.

Behind me, I can hear my grandmother Bianca yelling. Usually my it's my dad and mom, along with my little sister, but my mom, along with her friends are in the Bahamas for the week, taking a much-needed vacation. It's a toss-up between my grandma and my mom being the team's biggest fans. Both of them insist that they sit behind the bench while my dad prefers to sit in the luxury suite. I get where he's coming from. He gets tired of the security always around him. He wants to enjoy the game and not be hounded by fans all the time.

But my mom wants to be where the action is, and since they're ridiculously in love, my father does whatever she wants. In turn, he tries to please my grandmother as well. They had a rocky relationship right up until my sister was born, but now they're close and she's making up for lost time.

My sister, Betty Paige, sits in between my dad and grandma with her nose tucked into a book. She has no desire to be a football fan, but my parents are adamant that she comes each weekend to support me.

Sometimes Nick and Aubrey, along with their two kids Mack and Amelie make the trip to Portland. It's usually when the high school football team has a bye weekend. He's still coaching and often asks my dad to help, especially with Mack playing now too. Nick and my dad are friendly, but will never be best friends. He saves that title for Harrison James and Jimmy Davis, his two band mates, both of whom are living in Los Angeles, far away from Beaumont.

Jimmy and Jenna, along with their daughter Eden chose to move to California after Harrison's sister got married there one winter. Jenna fell in love with the beach and didn't hesitate to pack up and move. Eden is some junior surfing champion or something like that and from what Quinn tells me, it drives Jimmy crazy.

With Quinn going to college in California and Elle following him, Katelyn wanted to be there even though Peyton decided that Northwestern in Chicago was more her speed. She's making a name for herself while in school being a sports reporter and apparently has job offers pending from every sports channel out there.

Once I left for college, I came home as much as my schedule would allow. Most of the time my parents came to Indiana for the holidays and sometimes Peyton would come with them. I think, deep down, my parents knew that I needed to see Peyton more than Elle or Quinn. She's my best friend, my confidant and there isn't anything I wouldn't do for her. When I was able to go home, it was rare that I would run into Quinn. After he graduated high school, he took off to Los Angeles and immersed himself in the music scene. I do, however, have every single song of his and am probably his biggest fan, minus the large contingent of women that he has following him around. It's been a few years since we were all together and truthfully, I miss the group. I miss having everyone around. When we're together, we're inseparable, a tight-knit group and right now we're spread all over the place.

I suppose the next big gatherings will be someone's wedding and if my girlfriend, Dessie, has her way about it, it'll be ours. I'm not there yet, but she is. She's all about what everyone thinks and her fellow Victoria Secret models are telling her that she should have a ring already. Personally, I don't see anything wrong with waiting, with making sure that marriage is the right step.

I stand on the sideline with my hands gripping the neck of my jersey while I watch our defense give up yard after yard. The closer the opponent gets to the end zone the more my ass is puckering. If they score, the game is over. Their quarterback is seasoned and knows how to bleed the clock making sure that we'll have no time left.

We hold them on the forty and I groan when they send their kicker out. He's one of the best in the business and hasn't missed this year. Still, I stand there next to Bud and watch as he lines up and prepares to kick.

The ball is hiked, he starts his motion and his foot connects with the ball. Sure enough, it flies through the uprights as the clock expires. I hang my head as people pat me on my shoulders and tell me good game.

Good isn't enough. Not in my book. I want to win. I want the city to be proud of their football team. I want players to want to come here, to play here and make our team stronger and that isn't going to happen if we don't start winning.

After giving the other team congratulations, I head to the bleachers where my family is waiting.

"Good game," Paige says, even though she doesn't mean it.

"Did you watch, Little B?"

She shakes her head and shrugs sheepishly. At twelve she'd rather read, shop, and pretend that she isn't crushing on Mack Ashford.

"Tough loss," my dad says as he reaches out to shake my hand. "The clock--"

"Yeah, coach said the same thing. I'll work on it."

"Well, I thought you were great," my grandmother says.

My dad and I look at her and shake our heads. "You're supposed to say that because you're my grandmother."

She waves her hand dismissing both of us. That's one thing Bianca Westbury doesn't do, she doesn't sugarcoat. I love her, but she has no filter. I think that is why she and my mom get along so well. My mom doesn't hold back either.

We like to give my mom a hard time about how she reacts. During the game, she cusses like a sailor and threatens bodily harm if she feels like I'm not being protected. But when she's talking to me, she's sweet and syrupy, telling me that everything is okay. My dad calls her the Jekyll and Hyde of sports mothers. My grandmother is the same.

"I'll meet you guys at the hotel. I need to shower and go pick up Dessie."

After a quick team meeting and a shower, I'm home and walking into the arms of Dessie. She's usually at my games unless she has to work. She spent the last week in Costa Rica shooting a spread for a swimsuit catalog that will be out this spring.

"Sorry about the loss," she says into my shoulder. I breathe her in and am instantly relaxed. "Was it because I wasn't there?"

Oh how easy that would be. I laugh and pull away from her. "No, just wasn't our game to win," I tell her. "Are you ready to go to dinner with my family?"

She nods, but her enthusiasm doesn't exactly meet her eyes. Dessie is convinced that my mother doesn't like her. I tell her that she's just being silly and that my mom loves everyone. I have never asked my mom if she likes Dessie or not and figured that if she has a problem with her, she'd say something. I don't bother telling her that my mom isn't here today because that might give her a false sense of security. Bianca Westbury's wrath is ten times worse than my mom's.

The hotel that everyone is at is only two blocks away from my apartment, allowing us to walk over. If it isn't my name being called by the people we pass, it's Dessie's. Rarely can we go out around town without someone noticing either of us. I guess it's a good thing when you think about it, and honestly, it's something I've been used to since I was about ten.

When we arrive, Paige opens the door. She's crying and one look at my dad tells me something is really wrong.

"What's going on?" I ask, causing my father to stop his frantic packing.

"It's Peyton."

"What about her?" I ask, reaching for my grandmother as she brushes past me with Betty Paige's bag.

"She was in a car accident, Noah. Harrison says they don't expect her to make it. We have to go to Chicago."

"Wh-what?" I ask, swallowing hard. My tongue feels thick and foreign in my mouth, while my stomach rumbles.

My dad shakes his head. "I've called for a chartered flight. Your mom... they're on their way from the Bahamas now on the band's plane."

"Harrison?"

"Chartered a flight with Elle, Quinn, JD and Eden. They're all coming."

"I'm coming with you," I say. My dad doesn't say anything because he already knows that is where I need to be.

"Noah?" Dessie says my name quietly. I look at her and she shakes her head. "We have plans."

I close my eyes and process what she's saying. "My best friend has been in an accident. I have to go to her." I look deep into Dessie's eyes, looking for any sign that she understands what I'm saying.

"...It's always about Peyton."

She's right. It is. She's all I'm going to think about because this can't be happening to her. It's all I can think about as I storm out of the suite when I was ten and my uncle Mason was killed. This can't happen to Elle and Katelyn, not again.

HOLDING ONTO FOREVER
THE BEAUMONT SERIES - NEXT
GENERATION
OCTOBER 12, 2017

PRE-ORDER HERE:
AMAZON
BARNES & NOBLE
IBOOKS
KOBO